THE GOOD ONE, PART 2

THE HAPPY ENDINGS RESORT SERIES, BOOK 41

JENNIFER SIVEC

Edited by
JC WING

Illustrated by
JM WALKER

To all of us who feel the we can never be enough, you must understand that we have always been and will always be, the good one.

CHAPTER ONE

Olivia, Age Seven
  Molly, Age Fourteen

OLIVIA LIKED VINCE.

She thought he was handsome with his dark brown eyes and thick black hair. He spoke to her with a beautiful accent, and she knew that Molly liked him, too, because they were kissing all the time.

When Mommy was gone and Molly was supposed to be watching her, Vince snuck in to visit. Olivia knew that if Mommy knew she would be really mad so she was careful not to say anything.

Mommy didn't like anything Molly did, and she especially didn't want Molly talking to boys. When she thought Molly was talking to boys, she called her bad names that Olivia wasn't allowed to repeat.

Molly always told Olivia, "I'm old enough to have a boyfriend, Livvie Boo-Hoo. Don't tell that witch or she'll take Vince away from us."

Vince always brought Olivia gifts of candy and little stuffed animals that he knew she would like. Olivia liked Vince and didn't want Mommy to know about him. He was one of the nicest people she'd ever met.

On a boring Saturday night when Mommy was out at the bar with her friends, Olivia heard the special knock and knew that Vince was at the door. She opened it carefully, like Molly had taught her, and motioned for Vince to hurry inside.

"Hi, Munchkin!" he said, his teeth white and shiny as he lifted Olivia high in the air and gave her a hug. "How's my girl?"

Olivia giggled.

Vince was handsome, and she liked his smile.

He handed her a flower and a stuffed pink bear and winked at her.

"You spoil her," Molly said, kissing him on the mouth.

"Nah. She's my girl. I gotta take care of her, don't I?" Vince said, kissing Molly again for a long moment.

Olivia looked away, embarrassed. She smelled her flower and decided she liked it.

"Vince and I are going to read for a little while on my bed," Molly said as she grabbed him by the hand then led him toward the closed bedroom. "You stay in here and watch TV, but you can't bother us. Okay?"

Olivia nodded.

Anything Molly said, Olivia did.

Molly and Vince disappeared into the room, the door closing behind them.

Olivia wandered to the kitchen area and opened the cabinet where the cookies were. She grabbed a handful and set them carefully on paper plate, then sat down in front of the TV hugging her new soft pink bear. She ate her cookies slowly, opening them one by one and licking the cream inside. They were her favorite, but Mommy didn't buy them for her unless she was very good.

She savored each one, not sure when she would get them again.

She turned on the television and found her favorite show about the animals who were like superheroes and saved the world.

Before long, Olivia heard weird noises coming from the bedroom.

She heard Molly giggling, and that made her happy. She always liked when Molly was happy, which was never unless Vince was around. Vince was nice to Molly, and she hoped that he would be her boyfriend forever. The nicer Vince was to Molly, the nicer she was to Olivia.

Olivia took small bites of her cookie and chewed carefully, making sure she didn't leave any crumbs. Molly had been so angry with her lately, and she didn't want to give her any reason to be mad at her.

Messes always made Molly mad because she said that Olivia was selfish and spoiled.

Olivia wiped the tear from her eye as she remembered how Molly had pulled her hair the last time she had left crumbs on the floor. She'd apologized later, but Olivia had cried anyway. She'd forgiven Molly for hurting her because she always did.

Suddenly, the door to the trailer slammed open and Mommy stumbled in, her eyes red, mascara smudged all over her face.

Olivia's last cookie fell on the floor and she stared at it, frozen.

"Why are you sitting here watching TV by yourself?" Mommy slurred as she came closer to Olivia, the strong odor that Olivia didn't like permeating the air. Olivia knew that when she smelled like that, there always trouble that followed.

Olivia couldn't speak.

"Are you deaf? I asked you a question." Mommy's eyes were dark, and Olivia trembled inside.

Mommy reached out and grabbed Olivia's wrist, pulling hard. "When I speak to you, you answer, dammit."

Olivia heard a groan from behind the bedroom door, and she could feel Mommy's entire body stiffen.

The air in the trailer was electric as neither of them dared breathe.

Olivia heard it again, followed by another groan and the rhythmic sound of squeaking bedsprings.

It was faint, but Olivia knew by the way Mommy looked at the door with her mouth open that she had heard it, too.

Mommy leaned in closer to Olivia's face and hissed, spit flying out and landing on her cheek. "Who's in there? Is your sister in there?"

Olivia sat as still as she could, her heart pounding in her chest.

Mommy swore. "I told you to answer me when I speak to you!"

The blow to the side of Olivia's head was unexpected, and made her ears ring. Again and again, she could feel the slapping coming at her in the same place, hard and fast.

Dazed and dizzy, she watched as Mommy kicked open the door, and for a split second, Olivia could see in the room.

All she could see was naked skin and then Molly as Mommy grabbed her long strawberry blonde hair and threw her out of the room. Molly was almost naked, only wearing a short, thin T-shirt.

Vince jumped up and gathered his clothing quickly, and Olivia realized that he was completely naked. She had never seen a naked man before and felt her cheeks turn red as he scurried to put on his underwear and avoid Mommy's blows, her fists landing on him clumsily.

She had been too preoccupied with Molly.

He barely escaped as he ran out of the front door as fast as he could.

"Is this what you do when I'm not home? You whore around with that boy in front of your sister?" Mommy screamed at Molly, her words garbled in Olivia's ears.

Olivia reached up to the side of her head where Mommy had kept hitting her and gingerly touched her sore ear. It was wet inside, and when she pulled her fingers away she saw redness on the tip of her finger.

Blood!

She pulled her finger away and tried to wipe the blood on the floor where no one would see it. Mommy didn't like when she complained after she hit her, and she knew that saying it hurt could end up making things worse.

She watched as Mommy grabbed Molly's arm and then yanked her toward her, hard.

"How dare you have sex in my bed with that disgusting boy?" Mommy's face was red as she called Vince a lot of ugly words that made Olivia shrink inside. Mommy said words like that when she talked about anyone who had a different skin color than they did.

Olivia didn't understand why Mommy didn't like people who looked different than they did, and it made her squirm.

Vince had always been nice to her, and she didn't like anyone saying those ugly words. Especially not Mommy.

She shrunk down and hugged her knees as she watched Mommy grab Molly by the arm. Molly was sobbing and her face was red.

"You want to show everybody your perfect little body?" Mommy yelled. "If that's what you want, then that's what we'll do!" She dragged Molly to the door, even though Molly tried to squirm away. Mommy's grip on her arm was tight, and Olivia could see the red marks already forming on her sister's forearm.

Olivia could see that Molly didn't have any underwear on, her thin white T-shirt left nothing to the imagination as Mommy opened the door to the trailer and threw Molly out, not bothering to see if she landed safely.

Olivia heard Molly land with a thud and a scream.

Mommy slammed the door and locked it. She stood still for a moment then quickly grabbed a large bowl from the cabinet and filled it with water. She opened the door and threw the water at Molly as Molly screamed again, her sobs coming through the door as she begged to be let in.

Olivia couldn't stop crying, her head hurting, a hollow feeling in her right ear. She reached up and felt wetness on the right side of her face and knew it must be the blood again, but she didn't care.

She lay on the ground and closed her eyes, the sound of Molly's cries echoing in her ear.

Olivia felt dizzy, like she was going to throw up, and when she closed her eyes she hoped, not for the first time, that she wouldn't have to open them ever again.

CHAPTER TWO

Olivia, Age Thirty-Five

The Split

THE NOTE in his front left jacket pocket that told him that he was her world didn't surprise me. It was almost as though he had left it there purposely, hoping I would find it and put an end to the pointless dance we had been doing for the past few years.

I wasn't even angered by it, even though the world threatened to stop turning as I read them.

I wanted to hate him, but I hadn't felt anything in years; the medication I'd promised to take numbing me to the bone. The ability to be happy or sad or even angry escaped me when I needed it the most. The only love or joy I had was for the children.

I hadn't loved him in so long, and the nineteen-year-old

girl who had fallen in love with him didn't even seem like she'd ever been me. We were fulfilling a sense of duty to a marriage that was dead, at our very best, and I wondered why it had taken him so long to find someone else.

"I'm sorry you had to find out that way," Danny said, unapologetically.

"How did you meet?" I asked, emotionless.

"In a coffee shop. She'd forgotten her wallet and I..."

"Had to be the hero," the words had come out harsher than I'd intended, but I understood because he'd been saving me throughout our entire life together. I shouldn't be surprised that it was another damsel in distress who had caught his eye. If he had a red cape and a big "S" on his chest, I couldn't have been more surprised.

"I didn't mean for this to happen, Livvie," Danny said, suddenly ashamed, the boy I'd once loved reappearing for a brief moment.

"I know," I said, believing him.

He had been a stranger for so long; the bright-eyed young man who'd once held me close when I was terrified or had a bad dream had disappeared long before. I had killed him, destroying the last remnants of him with my constant need to be saved.

"Do you love her?" I asked, already knowing the answer.

He didn't answer, his eyes refusing to meet mine.

Danny cleared his throat. "You and I... haven't been us for so long, and I felt like I could never leave. I know there's no excuse for what I've done. If I hadn't been such a coward, I would've just left and let us both move on. There was a time when you were my world but now..."

His voice trailed off, and I knew what he wanted to say but was afraid to.

It was all too much.

Even for a guy like Danny who had a hero complex and a strong heart, my illness suffocated us both. I'd done everything I could in the beginning when the babies were small, but everything unraveled quickly, over and over, until I'd worn us both down into nothing.

It was the endless doctor's appointments when the medication stopped working and the constant checkups even when it was. It was the mania and the depression and then the forgiveness that I'd begged him for but didn't deserve because of what I'd done to the children... and to him.

It had all been too much, and I knew that he had to break one day.

I sat on the side of the bed and watched him pack, willing my heart to feel something and my mouth to open because I knew that I should beg him to stay.

For the children.

For me.

But I sat in silence, watching him open drawers as he painfully decided what to take and what to leave. The note had sealed the deal for both of us, making his alternate life a reality, but he was never going to stay. He'd made his decision months before, even searching out condos and apartments and finally settling on one that was close to the children but far enough away from me.

I watched as he closed the final suitcase, and I knew that I should feel something as he clicked it closed. I waited for the pang of emotion, the sense of dread, the panic to set in, but there was nothing.

Absolutely nothing.

"I'm not a bad guy, Livvie." Danny looked me directly in

the eye, both of us dry-eyed and listless. "We had something incredibly special once. Please don't forget that. I know that I never will."

I nodded as I watched him walk out of the room. I'd opened my mouth to speak but no words had come out as I realized there was nothing I could say that would have any meaning.

I watched from behind the curtain of our bedroom window as he packed up his car. I knew that I was standing only by sheer will and wondered briefly when my legs would finally decide to give out.

I was the only one who would be shocked that we were finally splitting up, everyone else surrounding us wondering why it hadn't happened sooner. There was the constant fighting, the silence, the tension, and the bitterness swirling around us where love had once been.

We'd already agreed upon what we would tell the kids, and we knew that they might even be relieved. Our house had become a tomb where joy lay dormant and happiness only occurred when one parent was absent and the other one was home.

We had separated long before the moment he emptied his dresser drawers into his suitcases. I imagined she would live there, too, though I didn't want to think about her.

I didn't even want to think about him any longer.

He'd stayed because he was afraid that I couldn't handle him leaving, but now he didn't have a choice. He was too far down the rabbit hole, and I'd been stable for long enough so it was now or never, and he'd chosen now.

The kids were going to be alright. We both knew it.

We adored them, and in turn, they loved us, separately and not together. Together we were nothing, but separately we had become everything, and I knew that this was the right thing for us. The only time I felt alive was when I was with them, my heart bursting for their every smile and laugh. They deserved happiness. I wanted them to see what love could be instead of the emptiness of our hands that never held one another's, or the coldness of our lips that never touched.

If Danny and I couldn't show them that, then maybe Danny and his new love could.

I wanted it to be more painful than it was, but I'd conditioned myself over the years to be more in control so that I wouldn't fall apart. The intensive therapy had helped me with that, and the medication numbed the rest.

Even though Danny and I had been so much in love so many years before, I could no longer feel it. I only remembered it as though it had happened to someone else entirely. I recalled the love because he told me that it had once been there, but I still felt nothing.

I remembered the beginning when he barreled into me on that staircase at school and accidentally broke my wrist. I remembered every detail, just as I knew that I would remember every detail of the moment when he left.

The vividness of the blue shirt he had been wearing, the crease in his forehead when he told me he was leaving, the flatness of his voice as he told me that he would always look out for me.

Even the self-loathing and regret that he exuded when he realized that I knew what he'd done.

He had been my Danny, and I knew that I would remember it all but not as a passenger, merely as an observer. My heart had been empty for so long that I'd forgotten it was supposed to be full.

And just like Molly, without permission or warning, he was out my life, and I had been powerless to stop him.

Just like Molly, when he left, I was alone.

Just like Molly, I didn't know if I would be able to survive, even though I told myself that I always had and always would, even if it meant that I was completely on my own.

CHAPTER THREE

Olivia, Age Seven
  Molly, Age Fourteen

ONE MONTH later

EVER SINCE THE night when Mommy had found Vince and Molly, things were drastically different.

Molly had disappeared for a month but finally returned, not telling Olivia where she had been. She no longer spoke, not even to Olivia.

For the first time in her life, Olivia was alone, hiding in the shadows, waiting for Molly to notice her and care for her like she had promised.

The ringing in Olivia's ears had stopped, but no matter how hard she tried, she realized that she couldn't hear out of that ear anymore. She'd mentioned it several times, but there was no doctor visit and nothing was done, so she grew accustomed to the hollowness in her bad ear.

The world had grown quieter, but she grew used to hearing the things she wanted and ignored the things she didn't. This was useful, especially in school when teachers tried to call on her but gave up.

Their confusion with her new disability was evident but overlooked because her classroom was over-crowded, and her school under-funded. Olivia wasn't any trouble so they left her alone, which she preferred.

Her deafness became her superpower, and Olivia learned to use it to her advantage.

The world had changed and without Molly, Olivia didn't need anyone other than Ben, her best friend. He was the small, quiet boy who lived in the trailer next to theirs. He often hid outside with her when his parents started yelling too loud, and things began to crash against the walls inside of his tiny trailer that looked just like hers.

He was her only companion and the only one who understood her. They tightly clung to each other's friendship, thankful for another soul who recognized the pain.

His deep sorrowful eyes were the same ones she saw in the mirror every morning when she brushed her teeth without anyone telling her to. Ben and Olivia were one and the same, two sides of the same battered coin.

After the night when Mommy found Molly and Vince, Olivia felt she no longer existed to anyone.

When Molly came back home after the month of being gone, she was a ghost. Her return had been uneventful, and even though Olivia had met her at the door with excitement and happiness, Molly ignored her, not saying anything as she entered the trailer quietly.

Mother had looked at Molly with a blank stare, and then lit another cigarette.

"I'm only letting you back because if I don't, they'll

arrest me for being 'neglectful'," Mommy had told her, not even looking in her direction. "But if you have that boy in here again, I swear, I'll kill you both. I'm not having you get pregnant!" Molly hadn't said a word as she opened the door to her room and disappeared. Olivia's excitement disappeared as quickly as it came, a sickening feeling in the pit of her stomach replacing it.

Molly had been skinny and dirty, and Olivia knew that she was staring at a stranger instead of her sister.

It was a Sunday, four weeks after Molly had returned home when Olivia knew that something was terribly wrong.

The smoke in the trailer was especially thick that day, with Mommy's newest man friend just leaving. Olivia hid under the dining table, careful not to kick the leg out, doing her best to avoid him. He was just like the rest. Fat and sloppy with bloodshot eyes that lingered on her far too long. She had pretended to be invisible until he left so that he couldn't see her, even though she knew he did.

When Molly banged open the door and walked in the trailer, Olivia hid even further under the table. Molly had been gone for several days, Mother not even questioning where she had been.

"It's one less mouth to feed," she had told Olivia as she'd thrown a Hot Pocket onto a plate and handed it to her the night before.

Molly's long hair was knotted and greasy, and there were dark circles under her beautiful eyes. Her clothes looked like they belonged to someone much bigger, hanging off of her unusually thin frame, and Olivia immediately wondered when she's eaten last.

She didn't even look in Olivia's direction, her gaze fixated on Mommy, burning with anger.

"Because of you, you bitch, no matter how hard I try,

Vince refuses to even talk to me!" Molly yelled, her eyes rimmed with red.

Olivia shrunk into the corner and drew her knees to her chest, her heart pounding loudly in her ears. She wanted to look away but couldn't, suddenly afraid of the stranger that had become her sister.

Mommy took a long drag of her cigarette and blew out the smoke without take her eyes off of Molly. "Why do you think I would care? You and that ... animal ... in my bed with your sister just outside the door, is disgusting. *You're* disgusting! Jesus, look at you! You're just a filthy little whore, just like I always knew you'd be."

"Then I must take after you!" Molly shot back.

Olivia moved quickly, anticipating what would come next. She threw herself into the corner behind the side of the couch, nearly gagging from the stench of it. This had been her hiding place since she was much younger. She imagined that it protected her from what was sure to come, though she knew it likely wouldn't.

Mother stood up. She moved much faster than she looked like she could, her face two inches from Molly's.

"I'm not afraid of you," Molly said unmoving. "I'm not afraid of you anymore. You can't hurt me because there is a baby growing inside of me, and thanks to you, it'll grow up fatherless just like I did."

Mommy froze.

For a moment an expression came over her face that the sisters had never seen, and Olivia thought she looked almost pretty, her eyes instantly soft.

But in a split second it was gone, and Olivia wondered if she had even seen it at all.

"You're pregnant!?" Mommy asked, sticking her finger in Molly's chest.

"It would seem that way," Molly said, defiantly.

"How do you know for sure?" Her eyes scanned Molly's body.

"I know. Vince's mother paid for a pregnancy test, and when it came back positive she demanded that he do the right thing, but he refused." Molly took a deep, ragged breath. "He said he didn't want anything to do with my crazy family. He said 'I'm not having a baby with some crazy bitch'." Molly cried out, her brown eyes overflowing with tears. "It's all your fault. You scared the shit out of him!"

"I knew you would get yourself knocked up," Mommy's voice was hard as she took a step back from Molly. "I knew that it was only a matter of time."

"I loved him!" Molly cried. "He was the only thing in this shithole place that made anything worth a goddamn. He made me happy and now... now he hates me."

"What did you expect when you opened your legs to a piece of trash like him? Did you really think he was going to take you away from all of this?" Mother laughed, the smoke of too many cigarettes rattling in her lungs. "Men are all the same, girls." Mother looked right at Olivia. "They'll use you and leave you. They're just in it for themselves so I don't wait for anyone. I learned that from your piece-of-shit father!"

"He was different! He loved me until you tossed him out without his clothes... he loved me." Molly's eyes were hard as she stared at her mother.

"No, you stupid girl. He's the same as the rest of 'em. If he was so different he never would've have gotten in your pants when your baby sister was only a few feet away. He just cared about getting in your..."

"Why is everything always about Olivia? Do you even care that I'm pregnant?" Molly screamed.

Mommy's eyes turned dark, and Olivia covered her eyes. She'd seen that look before, and suddenly she felt as though she couldn't breathe.

She watched in horror as Mommy punched Molly in the stomach. Molly hadn't been expecting it and went to the floor with a thud. Olivia closed her eyes tight, terrified to open them, but she knew from Molly's cries that she was in pain. She felt like she was going to throw up and wanted to help her, but she knew all too well that there was nothing she could do.

"No!" Molly screamed. "Don't hurt my baby! Not my baby!"

Mommy punched Molly again hard, and then one more time until Molly doubled over.

Molly's cries clung to Olivia's good ear until they finally turned into quiet moans.

Suddenly, there was silence, and Olivia's body shook as she held herself tight. She was afraid to open her eyes, afraid of what she would find. After a few long moments she heard the creaking of the trailer door open, then close and lock.

She was terrified to move and wondered if it was Molly or Mommy who left. It was as though they'd forgotten that she was even there, and she was frightened to breathe.

Finally, she heard a groan, and she poked her head out to see Molly's feet.

"Molly," she whispered, cautiously. "Molly... are you okay?"

There was no answer.

Olivia crept carefully from behind the couch and crawled on the floor toward Molly's feet that remained still.

'Molly, Molly." Olivia's voice was broken.

"Olivia..." Molly's voice was weak, and Olivia felt herself breathe for the first time, terror clutching at her throat.

Olivia crawled to her sister afraid of what she would find.

She gasped at the sight of her. Even though she had seen bruises before, she forced back tears. Molly's face was covered with smeared blood that was coming from her nose, a purplish bruise beginning to spread across the entire right side of her face.

She lay on her side, unmoving.

"Are you okay?" Olivia tried not to cry. "What can I do?"

Molly opened her mouth but nothing came out. Olivia gently grabbed her hand and held it.

"Please... what can I do?" Olivia tried to sound brave. They had always been there for each other after one of Mother's rages, but this was far worse than she had ever seen.

"Nothing..." Molly choked out. "Nothing. Get away from me. You can't help me! Please."

Olivia looked at her helplessly. As Molly straightened out her legs, she realized in horror that Molly's jeans were covered in blood. As the redness grew over her thighs, Olivia began to shake.

"What's happening?" she cried out. She was afraid to ask if she was dying, but she knew she must be with all of the blood.

"She killed it." Molly's voice was weak. "She killed my baby."

Olivia, Age Forty-Five

· · ·

MY PHONE BUZZED, and I leaned over to see who was texting me at such an ungodly hour.

It was the neighbor, Clay.

He was the perfect neighbor, always lending tools and helping to fix things around my house that needed repair. Me without a husband and him without a wife, both divorced and lonely, we had managed to create a situation where neither of us had to be alone if we didn't want to be. He was handsome and kind and on occasion funny. But no matter how many times I told him that I didn't want to be involved with him on a serious level, he still tried.

"Good morning!" the text said, as it did every morning for the past month.

I sighed.

The phone buzzed again.

"I just wanted you to know I was thinking about you."

I ignored it like it often did.

I wasn't trying to be cruel, but I didn't want to lead him on, and he couldn't seem to understand that I didn't want to take our relationship to the next level. He was under the impression that it was the next step but I didn't want that.

When I looked at him, all I thought was that he wasn't Danny, and I didn't want that for him. Or for me.

Occasionally, I answered his texts, carefully and briefly, but today I didn't respond as I placed my phone in the drawer of my nightstand so I wouldn't have to look at it and feel guilty.

I liked him, but I didn't want him. He had nice hands and a soft mouth that sometimes got too sloppy as he got more excited, but he was tolerable, and that was all I wanted. I wanted tolerable and easy to ignore, and he was both of those things. He wanted more but I'd told him that I never would, yet he refused to stop trying.

I sighed.

I laid back against the soft pillows and closed my eyes. I didn't want him to think about me. I only wanted what I wanted from him and nothing more.

I was never going to love him, and I'd told him so time and again but he didn't believe me.

"You will one day," he always said, hopefully. "I promise you will."

I'd never even let him sleep over, always making him leave, careful not to spend more time with him than was necessary. I had been honest with him about what I wanted but he continued to stick around, confident that I would change my mind one day.

My life with Danny had been over for over a decade, and nothing that I could do was ever going to change that. It was too late, but I still missed him every single day. Some more than most. Most more than some.

I closed my eyes and squeezed them tight, willing my heart rate to slow down and to normalize. I had been working on regulating my anxiety for many years and almost had it down to a science. The therapy, the meds, and the breathing. It all helped on most days.

Most.

I pressed my fingers against my temples and tried to push Danny out of my mind.

He slowly began to disappear, then suddenly the image of a dark haired boy flashed across my mind, and I felt like I had been punched in the stomach.

Chase!

Panic began to settle in as I wondered if he was cold, or hungry, or ... dead.

Mommy loves you, baby. She thinks about you every moment of every day.

It had been months since we've seen or heard from him. It was the longest we have ever gone without knowing where he was, and every day was a fresh hell as I waited to find out if he was still alive.

The police had stopped looking, believing that he'd run away but I hadn't. We had checked everywhere we could. We had scoured every inch of our town even going as far as Happy Endings, which was a few towns over and the hell-hole place where I had grown up.

We had tried searching everywhere with no luck. Even though our marriage had been over long before Chase disappeared, we still searched together, committed to finding our son.

Even though he loved someone else now, Chase was his son, and she understood our need to find him, together.

She was someone normal who made him happy in a way that I never could. She didn't need medication and therapy and wasn't off-balance like I was. She baked cookies from scratch and had a law degree from a prestigious university but worked for a non-profit. She was pretty and had tried hard to make me like her, even though I never would and had told her so.

In a sad way I was happy for him, knowing that he deserved to be happy. She wasn't the coffee shop girl, but someone else entirely different, and there was no reason for me not to like her. She'd done everything in her power to show me that she didn't judge me and that she wanted our relationship to be amicable. Losing our family had been my fault, everything I had put our family through had been too much.

Even someone as patient and perfect as Danny could never be expected to endure what I had put us through.

"I'll love you forever," he'd said, but forever had been

too long and too difficult, and I had destroyed the man he'd once been.

When I had been pregnant with Jill, I had begged him to help me, and we were able to pretend that we were happy for several years after that. I'd even believed it, falling in love with my baby and becoming human once again.

Jill had been my saving grace.

Even though she was the child I'd never wanted, she had brought me back to life with her chubby cheeks and soft skin. When she laid her head against mine, there was nothing wrong with the world anymore. While my memories of Molly were never far from my mind, Jill's love was a salve that healed me when nothing else could.

She made me believe that I could be a good wife and mother and live a normal life even though I still I lived in fear every day. I was petrified of the monster inside of me that scratched at the windows and doors struggling desperately to get out.

While Danny did everything he could to slay him, it wasn't up to him.

It was up to me, so I fooled myself into believing that everything was better and that we were safe. For a few short years after Jill was born we were truly happy. We were the perfect family, but I always felt like I was looking at them from the outside in; our perfect picture with the monster in the background.

I tried to love Danny as much as I could, but there was a limit to what I could give.

It was easier to be a mother than it was to be a lover.

Jill, Chase, and Ben drew it out of me, and being a mother was far more natural than I could've imagined. Maybe it was their tiny voices or inquisitive and innocent minds, but I was able to find wonder and amazement in everything they did. Even though I was a lousy wife, I did my best to be a loving mother.

When Jill turned ten and Chase was twelve and Ben was fourteen, our once quiet resentment turned into exploding battles of will, Danny finally fighting for the one thing he deserved but never got.

Love.

He was adamant and demanding that I love him the way he deserved, the way I was unable to. He was going to stop at nothing until he received the love he wanted.

The love he deserved.

Even if that meant that it was no longer with me.

CHAPTER FOUR

Olivia, Age Seven

"MOLLY, TALK TO ME. PLEASE!" Olivia shook Molly helplessly, tears cascading freely down her small face. "Molly! Please!"

Molly's eyes fluttered open at the sound of Olivia's voice, but closed again. Olivia squeezed her hand hard trying to ignore it as Molly's face grew whiter, the redness continuing to spread over her clothes.

"Molly, wake up! Please." Olivia felt helpless as she grabbed a blanket and laid it on top of her sister. Molly lay still, barely breathing.

The door to the trailer suddenly banged open and Olivia jumped.

"Get away from her!" Mommy hissed at the man friend who had just stumbled in behind her. He closed the door clumsily, watching Olivia as he did so, a half-smile on his face that made Olivia's skin crawl.

"Molly's hurt! You need to help her!" Olivia yelled at Mommy, angrily. "Help her, now!"

"Shut up!" Mommy hissed, her nose inches from Olivia's. "You don't tell me what to do. Ever!"

Olivia cringed. She'd heard that sharpness in Mommy's voice many times but this time Molly wouldn't be able to help her.

"You're a stupid child and don't know anything! Molly is going to be fine," Mommy stared down at Molly, her eyes empty. "Your sister has never been anything but a pain in the ass, and now she went and got knocked up by that ... boy. Trust me, she's going to be just fine."

Without warning, the big man swooped down and picked Molly up, throwing her roughly on his shoulder.

Olivia stared up at him, her eyes large with fear.

"Where are you taking her?" Olivia asked, her heart exploding out of her chest as she watched Molly's lifeless body flopping around.

"We're going to take her somewhere else, a place where someone will get her some help. We can't get her help from here or I'll go to jail, and I ain't going to jail." Mommy leaned over, her nose inches from Olivia's. "You can't say anything, you understand?"

Olivia nodded.

She knew how it was supposed to go. She was never allowed to say anything and she dared not to.

"Is she going to be okay?" Olivia heard her own voice and it sounded so small. She wished she was bigger so she could grab Molly from the big man.

"Yes, child. I already told you. She's going to be fine as long as you don't tell nobody about any of this." Mommy placed her hand on Olivia's head, gently at first, but then Olivia felt the pressure as she began to squeeze.

"I won't." Olivia said, wincing from the pain of Mommy's nails as they dug into her scalp. "I promise."

She watched as the big man nearly fell out of the door with Molly still awkwardly slung over his shoulder, his hands on her behind.

"Please, just make sure she's okay." Olivia whispered, afraid of her own voice.

"You just be a good girl, Olivia, and everything is going to be just fine."

Olivia watched as Mommy followed the big man out and wondered if she was ever going to see Molly again.

She sat on the couch and looked down at the floor where Molly had been laying. There was a big red stain on the floor, and Olivia looked at it for a long time. She stood up and realized that her whole body felt like it weighed a thousand pounds.

I better clean it up so that Mommy doesn't get mad.

She searched for a clean washrag and emptied the dish soap onto it. She tried to make the water in the faucet as hot as she could stand it and ran the rag under it, carefully. Mommy had always told her to clean with hot water and never cared if it scalded her hands. She was glad that Mommy wasn't there to shove her hands in it this time.

She walked carefully to the spot on the floor and began scrubbing.

Olivia watched in horror as the stain seemed to get bigger the more she scrubbed. She kept running her rag in the water, but she had run out of soap and was only using the hot water. She scrubbed harder, her hands turning red, and was relieved to see that the stain was getting lighter. Her arms were getting tired as she kept rubbing the floor. After what felt like an hour, she finally gave up.

The stain was noticeably lighter.

She knew that Mommy wouldn't think it was good enough, but she had tried to make it look better and just wanted to go to sleep.

Her stomach rumbled and she realized that she hadn't eaten since breakfast. She looked in the refrigerator, but there was nothing to eat, the hunger gnawing at her from somewhere deep in her stomach. She opened the cabinets and pulled out a crumbled package of Ramen Noodles.

She pulled out the pan and some water and lit the stove. She was careful like she always was as she dropped the noodles in and waited for them to soften. She had cooked Ramen Noodles for herself many times. They were easy, and Mommy said they were cheap, and they filled her up. She reminded herself to tell Mommy that this was the last package, and she hoped that she would buy her more.

When the noodles were finally ready, she put them in a bowl and then carried them over to their tiny table. She ate slowly, savoring every noodle. She tried to stop herself from thinking about Molly and all of the blood.

Is Molly dead?

Olivia chewed slowly. She wondered what it meant that Molly was knocked up.

She'd heard someone say it before, but it didn't make sense. What did it mean when someone got knocked up, and why was there so much blood?

Olivia worried about Molly, like she always did. She knew that Mommy didn't like her and wondered if she would ever see her again.

When she'd finished her noodles, she washed the pan and then her bowl with hot water, then dried them and put them back in the cupboard. Then she washed and dried her fork and placed it carefully in the drawer and walked slowly to the couch. She laid down, her head on the arm, and pulled the blanket over her, straining to hear any sound that might indicate that Molly was home.

She missed Molly and the way she used to be. She tried to remember the last time Molly braided her hair or took her on a walk to the park and found that she couldn't. It had been a long time and it made her sad. A tear fell down her cheek, and she brushed it away impatiently.

"Molly, come home soon," Olivia whispered into the dark, her big eyes wide as she stared at the ceiling. She lay as still as she could, holding her breath and waiting.

She didn't know what she was waiting for but she waited anyway, alone and in the dark, like she had so many times before.

CHAPTER FIVE

Olivia, Age Forty-Five
Friday

IT WAS FRIDAY.

It was the day before we'd be driving Jill off to college. It's the last day that she would be the daughter who was living in my house. Now she'd be the last child who was off to college.

The third child.

The only girl.

The baby.

She was only going to be five hours away but it felt like another continent. How did it come to this already? It didn't seem possible because neither of us seemed old enough.

I can still see Jill as a two year old raising her little arms up to me, "Mommy, up! Up, peeze," she would say. "Up now!" She was demanding and hilarious, her unruly brown curls poking out in a hundred directions, refusing to be tamed. Her hair was just like her, wild and unflappable, and

I loved that about her and wished I could be more like her. She laughed at anything and everything and thought I was the best person she knew, next to her daddy and big brothers, who completely adored her.

She always asked to be picked up so I tried to, but many chances passed me by, moments I'll always regret. I tried to carry her everywhere until I couldn't anymore, both of us disappointed when she had gotten too big. She would lay her little head against my shoulder, the softness of her hair finding its way to my cheek, my lips always finding her head. She was my world, and now she would be gone, living in a dorm room hours away, no longer in my house where I could see her bright smile every day.

I didn't know what I'd do without her. If was difficult taking Ben to college, but that had been nothing compared to her. She was the glue. She kept things light and normal, and with her gone, everything was about to change.

I knew how much Danny must be struggling too, even though we didn't talk about it.

We didn't talk much anymore, our communication focused only on the kids. Our conversations were short and sporadic, awkward and painful with words that went unsaid and emotions that were unexpressed. We were careful and cautious on the phone, afraid to say too much or too little.

"928" was long forgotten, the silver medallion necklace that Danny had given me for our first anniversary was now tucked safely away in my jewelry box, unworn for many years.

We hadn't seen each other in weeks, our only connection the kids and our search for Chase. Losing him had taken its toll on both of us, and I knew that he blamed himself. We both did.

"Maybe if I had tried harder, or if I had stayed," he'd

said on more than one occasion. "Maybe if I hadn't left, he would still be here with us."

I could tell in his eyes every time he looked at me that he had never forgiven himself.

"It's not your fault," I'd told him countless times. I always knew that it was mine but I couldn't convince Danny any differently.

We were irrevocably broken.

Divorce had been inevitable but I still missed him, even after all this time.

I knew that I would have to see him the next day, and my stomach was in knots.

Seeing him face to face was always unnerving, and I had made an extra appointment with Dr. Sullivan for the week.

Friday had snuck up so quickly, and I tried to take long deep breaths to calm myself and prepare for the next day.

"She'll be okay if we are okay, Livvie," Danny had said weeks before, which was the last time I had seen him as we met for coffee to finalize our plans to take her to college and square away her finances. He still liked to check up on me to make sure that I was eating and doing okay.

"I know. I just don't know ... what we'll do without her. I don't know what I'll ... " I paused, not wanting to say what I knew would come out next. *I don't know if I can be okay.*

The look in Danny's eyes was familiar. It was the look that he used to give me when he wanted to reach out me, a soft expression that made the brown in his eyes seem to sparkle, giving him a strangely angelic appearance. He had been my angel numerous times, but he had grown tired of it and so had I. I hadn't needed a guardian angel ... at least I didn't need one now. But that was the only role he had ever known how to play, and now I wondered if he could ever do anything else.

The silence was unbearable, and my mind reached back trying to find a time when we had been happy. Had it been before the boys were born? Before Jill was born? When the kids were little, hadn't we laughed a lot? At least, I thought we had. But then the darkness overcame me and it had changed me.

He stared at me for a long moment, thousands of words still unspoken between us.

We had talked for an hour and then he looked at the time on his phone, and I knew that it our cue to finish up. He needed to leave, presumably to go back to his new girl-friend. He had been open with me about her but it didn't hurt any less. As we stood to leave, he leaned in close, my heart pounding as he came closer, and then he planted his warm lips on my forehead. As he walked away, I could still feel the tingle from his lips, and I wondered how he could still make my heart pound after all of these years.

He wasn't near often, but when he was, he had the same effect on me as the day I first met him. I had never told him how much I'd loved him and needed him, and now it was too late, our lives moving in different directions, tied together only by the children we shared.

On the night before we took our baby girl to college, I wanted to reach out to him. I wanted to call him and hear the sound of his voice.

I wanted him to tell me that I was going to be okay and that everything was going to be fine, that I was going to make it through this. I missed how comforting his voice was and how strong he sounded even when I knew that he didn't feel it. I was being selfish and I knew it, but I missed him more than I ever imagined that I could.

No amount of medication or therapy would ever change that for me, and I realized that I never understood how much I loved him until it was too late.

I had punished him far too much, so now I paid with my loneliness.

A familiar heaviness overcame my heart and I stifled a sob that died in my throat. I didn't want Jill to hear me. I didn't want her to worry about leaving me. She had already put college off for a year, afraid to leave me alone, but finally Danny and I convinced her that she deserved a chance to spread her wings. I had even taken her to see Dr. Sullivan to show her that I was healthy enough to be on my own.

I knew that I could never live with myself if Jill missed her chance to go to school at the college of her dreams. I hadn't been completely on my own my entire life, but I knew that I didn't have a choice. I had already caused her so much pain, and I didn't want to hurt her anymore.

Without her I was going to be even more lonely and anxious. I knew that I would shift my focus to always worried about finding Chase. I knew that I would never let my children go easily, and I dreaded knowing that a piece of my heart was missing.

The king-sized bed I slept in felt so empty, so I comforted myself by imagining that Danny still lay next to me. I hugged the pillow tight and pretended that it was him, my head on his chest as he stroked my hair as I fell asleep.

As I finally drifted off, I imagined that I could hear Danny say, as he did so many nights before, "I still love you, Livvie, 928. I hope you'll believe me one day."

CHAPTER SIX

Olivia, Age Seven

MOLLY DIDN'T COME HOME, and Olivia's stomach hurt from waiting for her.

"When is Molly coming?" she asked Mommy after the third day she was gone.

"I told you to stop asking," Mommy said, pulling me close. She smelled like stale cigarettes and beer and I squirmed to get away. "She'll come home when she's feeling better."

"When is that going to be?" Olivia's voice was strained, her face red as she tried hard to control her voice.

"It'll be when I say it is," Mommy said, pushing me away from her, hard. "You should be thankful to me for saving you. You weren't ready to be an aunt and worse yet, I wasn't ready to be no grandmother. This little shithole wouldn't be big enough for all of us... and guess who would have to go?"

Mommy stuck her finger in Olivia's chest as she half-smiled. Olivia took a step back and wondered where she would go if she wasn't allowed to live there anymore. She didn't like living in the trailer but she wasn't sure who could ever take care of her.

She knew that Mommy would never send her away, but she stayed quiet anyway to be safe.

She didn't want anyone to have to leave again.

Olivia waited as patiently as she could, the days turning into weeks until finally two months had come and gone. When Molly finally arrived, she was even worse than she had been when she came home from Vince's house.

Without a word, Mommy brought her home.

Olivia's heart leapt out of her chest at the sight of Molly, but the moment they walked in the door, she went straight to their bedroom and closed the door.

Olivia got up and walked to the door, hesitating with her hand on the door handle.

"Leave her alone, Livvie," Mommy warned. "She needs to be alone."

Olivia looked at Mommy angrily.

"I want to see her!" she said forcefully, without thinking.

Mommy looked at her, her eyes wide.

"What did you say to me?"

Olivia didn't cower.

She was angry. She had missed Molly and desperately wanted to see her and hear the sound of her voice.

"I said, I want to see her. I want to talk to her now." Olivia was shaking, but she didn't care. She'd missed her sister. She'd spent her entire life with her, and being alone had been worse than anything she'd ever experienced.

Mommy looked at Olivia, her eyes dark. She leaned over, her face inches away.

"It don't matter what you want. She isn't ready to talk to you or anyone else. I'm warning you, little missy. Leave her alone."

Olivia shuddered at the danger in Mommy's voice.

She nodded, but didn't agree as she sat quietly, coloring with her broken crayons.

She looked toward the door and wondered what Molly was doing, her heart pounding in her ears. Did Molly even miss her at all?

She thought about the baby and all of the blood.

She'd been having terrible nightmares and in them, she was holding a baby covered in blood, and Molly was dead.

Mommy hadn't told her anything, and she knew that even if she asked, she wouldn't get an answer.

She didn't even know if Molly still had the baby. She hadn't seen one but she didn't know where it would've gone. What happened to Molly's baby?

Olivia tried to figure it all out in her mind even though she knew there were things that she was too young to understand. All she knew was that she'd missed her sister, and now that she was home she knew that something wasn't right.

She tried to concentrate on the coloring pages but her eyes grew heavy and before she knew it, she'd fallen asleep with so many questions swirling around in her mind.

She awoke, startled, and tried to remember where she was.

Molly!

The first thing she heard was the sound of Mommy snoring as she listened intently for any sound of Molly.

Olivia stood up, careful not to make a sound. She crept carefully to Mommy and stared intently. Olivia wondered if she had been pretty once. She stared at her thin wrinkled lips and tried to picture them with lipstick on like the pretty women on television. Her eyebrows were smudged and she snored heavily as she slept in the chair. She'd never been that close to her when she was sleeping before, and Olivia was mesmerized.

She could see faint traces of someone who might have been pretty once, but as quickly as she saw it, it disappeared. Even though she tried to love her, it was often overshadowed with the fear that welled up inside.

She thought about how angry Mommy would be if she woke up and saw Olivia so close to her. She knew that she wouldn't like it at all as she took a few steps away. She tried to remember being a baby and cuddling with her, but no matter how hard she tried she couldn't. She didn't ever remember Mommy hugging or kissing her like she heard Mommies did with their kids. She'd seen lots of them do it when they were dropping their kids off at school, but her Mommy never did even though she always told her that she liked her the most.

As much as she wished that she was loved she wanted Mommy to love Molly. Molly needed it more than she did because she was sadder, and Olivia felt a prick in her heart for her sister.

She tiptoed over to Molly's door and tried the doorknob. She sucked in her breath with surprise when it opened.

As she opened the door, she heard the stifled sound of crying and knew immediately that her sister was suffering.

"Molly?" Olivia whispered, softly.

The crying stopped immediately and Olivia listened but there was nothing but silence.

"Molly? Are you awake?" Olivia tried not to make too much noise, worried that Mommy would hear her.

She strained to hear if Molly would make another

sound when suddenly she felt a sharp pain in her head as she was jerked backward.

"I told you to leave her alone!" Mommy's eyes bored into her as the rage across her face sent chills down Olivia's spine. She had only seen Mommy angry like that at Molly, but never at her. "Why don't you listen?"

Olivia fell backward, pulling the knob as the door closed with a loud thud.

"I-I-I'm sorry. I just wanted to see her and ask if she was okay. I just needed my sister," Olivia cried, shielding her head with her arms as she waited for the blows that would surely follow.

"Put your arms down, you stupid girl. I'm not going to hit you. I've spent enough time trying to cover for you two, and I can't keep explaining your damn clumsiness to those hospital people." Mommy lit a cigarette while Olivia felt gingerly for the tender spot on her head where her hair had been pulled.

"I didn't pull it that hard," Mommy said smacking the top of her head, making Olivia wince. "I'm going to turn over a new leaf and stop hitting you girls. It's just not worth it no more."

Olivia stared at her in disbelief.

"But don't go thinking that you can just do whatever the hell you want. Your sister learned that the hard way. If you disobey me, there will be consequences, and I know plenty of people who would not have a problem hurting a little girl. Do you understand me?" Mommy blew her cigarette smoke in Olivia's face as she spoke. She tried not to cough as she nodded, still confused about what was happening. "And by the way, did I tell you? My new boyfriend is moving in. Roger."

Olivia froze.

Roger was the one who had taken Molly away, and when he stared at her, he made her feel naked.

Olivia shook her head.

"You don't like my Roger?" Mommy asked, smiling. "He's the first man who's made me feel like a proper woman in a long time, and if you don't like him, I don't really care. He likes me, and he said that he really likes you."

Olivia's body suddenly felt cold as she pushed back the nausea that threatened to overcome her.

"Speak, little missy!" Mommy barked suddenly making her jump.

"I-I-I like him. He's fine." Olivia said, the words tumbling out of her mouth before she could stop them.

"Good. It's settled," Mommy said as though she'd given Olivia a choice. "He's moving in tomorrow."

Olivia nodded, pushing down the terror that threatened to choke her.

Molly. I need you.

She stared at the door helplessly and waited for Molly to know that she was afraid like she always used to, but the other side of the door was silent, and Olivia knew that nobody was going to save her now.

CHAPTER SEVEN

Olivia, Age Forty-Five
Saturday Morning

IT WAS SATURDAY.

I got out of bed at five am, unable to sleep. I tossed and turned most of the night. For a moment I wondered why Danny's side of the bed is empty but then I remembered that he no longer lived there and hadn't for a long time. I knew that the day ahead would be long and strange, so I put a pot of coffee on and added a little extra, hoping that being over-caffeinated would make the day more bearable.

I tried to ignore the back door leading to the driveway, but it kept calling me. I'd said goodbye to too many people in my life but this one was the hardest.

My baby.

You have to face it, Liv. You need to do it before Jill wakes up and sees you fall apart. Do it now, before it's too late.

I turned the doorknob slowly, knowing what I would

find outside. We had packed up Jill's blue Ford Focus the night before, but I knew that seeing the car in the light of day would make everything more real, and I wasn't sure that I could face that reality.

As I stepped outside, I saw her car in its usual place in the driveway, and my heart suddenly felt like it might explode into a million pieces. Seeing everything packed tight and neatly made me realize that Jill's entire childhood, wrapped up with all of my hopes and dreams, was over. I realized that from the moment she was born until now, everything was complete. Her childhood was over and so was everything I had held onto for the last nineteen years. With Chase and Ben it had been so much easier, because then I always had her. But now...

"God," I moaned as I bit my lip hard, trying to stop myself from crying out. I crouched down on the ground trying to hold myself together. I didn't want anyone to see me like this. I didn't want Jill or Danny to see me this way, trying to keep from falling into a thousand pieces.

I'd seen Dr. Sullivan the week before, and I'd begged her to help me.

"What if I can't, Doc? What if I can't do it? Then what will I do? I can't do that to my family again. They've been through enough." I had pleaded with her remembering the last time I couldn't do it.

"You can do this, Liv." She had written a strong prescription for tranquilizers, but I refused to fill it. I was on enough medication and didn't need anything else to keep my brain from being clear. I kept the prescription buried in my purse as a safety net, in case I changed my mind. I wasn't confident that I could do this on my own.

I looked at the car and bit my lip again, harder this time. I told myself that everything would be okay and that I would be okay. This isn't about me, I reminded myself, it's about Jill. This is her life now, and I need to be happy for her. *Don't ruin this for her, like you've ruined so many other things. Don't do it this time, Olivia!*

I walked slowly to the garage and looked for the stash of cigarettes I had hidden. Jill knew that it was there, but we pretended that I didn't smoke. It was easier not to argue about how smoking was bad for me and caused cancer, blah, blah, blah. As I lit one up and inhaled, I felt the calm washing over me slowly as the smoke filled my lungs. Smoking was the only thing that made me feel normal. It was the one thing that cleared my head and gave me perspective when I was the most upset.

Jill didn't like it, but that didn't stop me. She knew that it helped, and she was always supportive of anything that helped.

I heard footsteps and quickly crushed the cigarette out.

"Hello?" I said, hoping it wasn't Jill as I waved the smoke away, knowing that I would still smell like it.

"Liv!" Danny walked up the driveway and looked as exhausted as I felt. It was the same look that I had seen before many times, concern etched all over his rugged, handsome face, his beautiful brown eyes red and tired. I hadn't seen him in over a week, and the sight of him made my heart hurt in a way that only happened when he was around.

I fought the memories that threatened to break through and focused on the neatly and fully packed blue Focus.

"How are you doing, Livvie?" he asked cautiously.

"I'm okay," I said, looking into his eyes for as long as I could. "I promise."

"Good," he said, his eyes tearing up. "Good. I'm glad, I was worried."

Of course he would be worried. I had always given him plenty of reason to worry, and even now he was concerned about me when he had no obligation anymore.

We walked back toward the house and prepared for the long day ahead in silence, both of us anticipating with dread what the next twenty-four hours would bring. Danny busied himself by following Jill around the house we used to share and staying out of my way. As difficult as it was, I tried to forget he was there. He wasn't there for me, it was for Jill, I reminded myself repeatedly.

The house phone rang a couple of hours later and I picked it up, instantly warmed from the inside out as my oldest son's voice came through the receiver.

"Is the Squirt ready?" Ben asked without saying hello. Much like my best friend and the man he was named after, Ben loved adventure. Ben and Michael had moved to the other side of the country seven years before, leaving me completely alone. It hadn't been planned but Michael's job had given him a hefty bonus which they needed for their growing family and they couldn't help but agree.

"You'll be okay," Ben had assured me, trying to make me forget that they were my only living family. "We'll talk every day."

But Ben knew that I would be lost without them both, and even though we messaged regularly, it wasn't the same. He had left me like so many others had, leaving me with days when I didn't know if I could make it without him.

My son Ben had planned a backpacking trip in the mountains the year before with a group of friends and wasn't table to be home to send Jill off. She had chosen to go to a different college with a start date a week earlier due to freshman orientation, and was okay with her older brother missing her big send-off.

"Yes," I said, trying to sound cheerful. But I'm not ready.

"How about you? How are you, Mom?" Ben asked in a rare serious moment.

"I'm doing fine," I said, ignoring the fluttering of my heart and the shaking of my hands.

Ben paused, "You know that if you need anything, you can call and I will be there in a minute."

"Yes, baby," I said, a wave of guilt flooding over me. When the boys were young they had always been sweet and protective, and I loved that about them, but they shouldn't have to worry the way they did. Ben had fared well in spite of me, but Chase was a different story, and nothing I could do now could change that. He was a lost soul, and it was my fault completely.

The damage had been done, and I only had myself to blame.

I looked down at the long scar on the inside of my right wrist and cringed. It had faded a little over time, but it was still there, white and angry, an ugly reminder of my utter failure as a mother. "I don't want you to worry. Everything is going really well. I promise."

"Have you heard from Chase?" Ben asked, hesitation in his voice.

"No," I said, not able to disguise the crack in my voice, and I choked back a sob. "Have you?"

"No," he said. I know he was trying hard not to blame me, but the edge in his voice was hard to miss. He swore he'd forgiven me but I couldn't imagine how he could.

We chatted awkwardly for a bit longer until Jill came bounding down the stairs and grabbed the phone. She loved her brothers, and even though they had given her plenty of hell, she had given it right back. She had always been extremely close to Chase who was closest to her age, but had gotten a lot closer to Ben in the past few months.

Jill put him on speakerphone, so that we could talk together.

"Benja-MIN!" Jill said, her voice light and happy.

I was overcome with the memory of Jill, Chase, and Ben talking together as children, thick as thieves,

"Hi, Squirt," Ben's voice perked up at the sound of her voice.

They chatted happily for a few minutes and then Ben's voice grew serious.

"Are you ready for this, Jilly?"

"Yes!" Jill said, her voice full of excitement.

"I'm proud of you," Ben said, his voice thoughtful.

Jill looked at me, embarrassment creeping over her pretty features, a small blush spreading over her cheeks. I looked away and busied myself with putting away dishes, feeling ashamed. I was the reason Jill had stayed around an extra year. It hadn't been fair to her and Ben knew it.

"I loved being home. I wasn't ready for college anyway," Jill said taking him off of speakerphone and walking out of the room.

I cringed inside as I poured myself another cup of strong black coffee. I swallowed it while it was too hot and cried out as the hot liquid burned the inside of my throat. I pushed back the tears that I knew were inevitable, not ready to release them just yet. Having Danny there and then talking to Ben had already made the morning trying. I wanted desperately to cocoon myself in my bed with the blanket over my head and disappear into nothingness.

I wiped away the few tears that had squeezed out and took a deep breath. I wished that I had filled that prescription for tranquilizers and then chastised myself mentally.

This was a part of life and I needed to feel it I reminded myself. I hated being numb even though it was the only way I had survived this far.

I had nearly lost everything. Molly. Ben and Michael. Danny. Chase. I wasn't ready to surrender anything else.

I took another deep breath trying to steady the desperation that was rising up in my chest and convinced myself for a few moments that everything was going to be okay.

I had survived losing Molly, I reminded myself.

I knew that I could survive this, too.

OLIVIA, Age Forty-Five
Good-Bye

THE FIVE-HOUR DRIVE felt like an eternity, and I wasn't sure how much longer I could take.

Danny was driving and barely going the speed limit, which made me crazy. He drove like an old lady on a Sunday morning any time the kids were with us, and this was no exception.

"Are you doing okay?" The text from Michael's phone made me smile. Michael had become just as much a part of my life as Ben was and they were nearly interchangeable.

"Danny is driving..." I responded, smiling at our inside joke.

"Uggggggggh. Hang in there!" Michael sent hearts. Ten of them, and I wished that they were here to hug me in person.

I wasn't sure if I wanted to scream or throw up, the tension and stress of the trip and what we were about to do eating me alive from the inside out. I wanted to scream or jump out of the car.

I wanted to throw myself in traffic.

"Daddy, can't you drive any faster?" Jill voice was high and anxious over the car speakers and I sympathized with her. She was excited about beginning her new life while we were trying to slow down time.

"We're driving as fast as we are going to," Danny said simply. "We'll get you there, Jilly. I promise."

"Oh Daddy," Jill growled as she hung up.

"You really could drive a little faster, Danny." I said, quietly.

Conversations about his driving were notoriously the same with exactly the same result.

"Liv, I don't want her driving too fast with a full car. You never know what will happen. We'll get there, I promise." Danny said patiently. Patience had always been one of Danny's strengths, one that Jill and I didn't share, but in this case, I needed all the time I could get.

I needed time to think and anticipate how I was going to say good-bye to my baby.

I reminded myself that parents do this all of the time. *This is what you were meant to do. This is what you are supposed to do. Being a parent is about letting go. Letting go.*

The reminder that nobody had driven me to college flashed through my mind, but I pushed it aside impatiently. It had been so long ago that I barely remembered it, or at least tried not to.

I repeated everything in my mind that Dr. Sullivan had told me. She had been preparing me for this moment for months, but I still didn't feel ready. I felt as though I was on the edge of a sharp cliff, getting ready to leap off. I didn't know if I could go home without Jill and I reminded myself that it wasn't an option.

"It's okay to feel the way that you do, Olivia but you have to do this for Jill. You have to keep reminding yourself that this is for her. You want her to be happy, don't you?" Dr. Sullivan had said in her low, soothing voice that sounded like slow-moving honey through my brain. I always wondered if she practiced her shrink-voice at home, or if it was just natural. Either way, I hated when she used that voice on me.

We approached the sign that said we were getting close. Only fifty-two miles until our destination.

I could see Danny's knuckles tense up. I snuck a look at him out of the corner of my eye desperately needing a distraction. His dark wavy hair needed a trim, which was typical. He rarely bothered with his appearance but didn't need to. He was gifted with good looks, the kind that were unintentional, but appealing.

The little wrinkles around his eyes and the gray in his temples were the only things giving away his age.

He was as good-looking as ever, even better-looking than when he was younger. Since I no longer saw him every day, the sight of him made my heart pound like it used to, a feeling that had been long-forgotten until now.

I had loved him so much back then but I had let him go, convincing myself that I was too tired to fight. Too tired to take my medication or go to therapy.

Instead, I had been selfish, and the regret stared back at me every day, reminding me that I was alone and had lost the love of my life.

"Are you checking me out?" Danny looked at me and teased, a small smile spreading across his lips.

"No," I said, embarrassed. "I was just thinking that you need a haircut."

He looked at me briefly and smiled, his smile not reaching his eyes. I wondered if he noticed that I'd put on a little weight and that I was finally eating fairly regularly, my cheeks were more filled out than they had been in years. Even if I had to choke the food down, I ate. I knew that I needed to in order to be healthy, and that Jill would notice if I wasn't. I hoped that I would continue eating with Jill away.

I didn't want to think about anything else as we quickly approached the college town with Jill who was practically riding our bumper.

As we pulled up to the campus, we found our way to where we needed to go. The campus was electric with frustrated parents and excited college-aged kids everywhere. The roundabout in front of Jill's dorm was a flurry of activity full of kids Jill's age and their parents. Everyone was unpacking little cars like hers, the kids clearly anxious to get started with their new lives.

Signs hung from windows that said "We'll take care of your daughter", and I could see the worry in Danny's eyes. We got out of the car slowly.

A kid about Jill's age walked by, and the vein in Danny's right temple began to pulse as the boy looked at Jill with more appreciation than was appropriate with her parents standing there. I put my hand on Danny's arm to steady him, but his jaw didn't relax.

Danny had protected Jill fiercely, mostly from me. It was my fault that she had seen more than most kids her age, but I wondered if we had shielded her too much from the dangers of the outside world.

Jill was my baby, but even more so, she was a Daddy's

girl. She had captured both of our hearts, so much so that we often jockeyed for her affections, wanting her to favor one of us more than the other. When it came down to it, she loved both of us, but she needed Danny and she protected me, and I hated that she worried about me at all, but I had given her good reason to.

"Daddy, I wish you guys were staying in town tonight," Jill said, looking down at the ground. We were sweaty and tired from moving boxes and furniture and in desperate need of a shower. We needed to get on the road, but we stalled as we stood there postponing the inevitable.

"I wish we could, Jilly, but I have to work early in the morning. It's going to be a busy day."

As much as I dreaded Saturday, I dreaded Sunday even more, and I wondered what I would do to quiet the chaos that would surely be floating around in my head. I knew that I would have to find a way. Dr. Sullivan had made me promise, for Jill's sake.

"Okay," Jill said, pausing as she bit her lip.

"Well, Liv. Are we ready?" Danny said, brightly, his eyes betraying his voice.

"Yes. I suppose. Is there anything else you need, baby?" I asked, cupping Jill's face in my hands.

For a brief moment, she was two, her face so young and cherubic with large blue eyes that always seemed to overcome her dainty face. I suddenly felt as though an elephant was sitting on my chest, and I realized that I was holding my breath, unable to breathe.

The moment had come to let her go, but I wasn't ready.

How could I ever be?

"Don't cry, Mom," Jill said, her husky voice suddenly serious. "Everything is going to be okay."

I hadn't even realized that I was crying, and I reached

up to feel the wetness on my cheek. It scared her when I cried, and I could feel Danny watching me out of the corner of my eye.

"I'm okay, Sissy," I said, wiping the tears away, embarrassed. Danny was right. If we were okay, she would be okay. I kissed her soft cheek and pulled her tight to me, breathing in the smell of baby powder and youth.

I stared at her, taking her in for the last time in a long time. She was an adult now. A beautiful adult.

I wondered where her baby fat and pigtails had gone and why they had to disappear so fast. Everyone said that she resembled me but I couldn't see it. I always thought she looked more like Danny, with her long legs and lean frame. Her dark hair was long and thick like mine, but wavy like Danny's. But her eyes, they were all mine. Deep blue, darker when she was angry, just like mine.

Love swelled up within me until I thought I would burst, and I walked away with tears in my eyes, my heart breaking in two as I fought the darkness that was chasing me.

"Oh, Mom," Jill said, hugging me tight. "It's going to be okay, Mom."

Suddenly, I could hear five year-old Jill's voice saying "It's okay, Mommy. Everything is alright."

She had been comforting me her entire life. Taking care of me since she was young, when I should have taken care of her instead. I wondered if she would ever forgive me for letting her down so much.

"If you hear from Chase..." Jill's voice caught and she couldn't finish.

"Of course," I said, barely able to say the words. His shadow hung over everything we did, and nothing significant could happen without us missing him. "I'll call you first thing."

Danny hugged us, and we all cried together, and for the first time in a long time, I didn't feel so alone. Aside from missing Chase, I realized that this was normal.

I was supposed to cry and lose it now, at the moment I was leaving my daughter at college. This heartbreaking, crushing feeling in my soul was how it was supposed to feel, and I realized that it felt good to be normal as I looked around at the other mothers and fathers who were crying, too.

We stood, holding one another, for what felt like a long time. We had been through so much, our little trio, especially since the boys had been gone.

Jill had been my lifeline, and I realized that it had always been this way. They had all saved me in one way or another, but Jill was the last, and I wondered how I would hold on without her now.

As though she was reading my mind, I heard her say, "You're going to be okay, Mom. You're going to be okay. You're so much better and stronger now. You have to remember that."

As we hugged each other one last time, I prayed that she was right and that my baby girl knew something that I didn't.

THE DRIVE HOME WAS SILENT.

My phone buzzed.

Clay.

"Are you okay? How did it go today?"

I regretted even telling him that we were taking Jill to college as I ignored the text.

He had acted jealous and possessive when I told him about it as though I should've invited him to go with us.

"Can't you just tell her about us before she leaves?"

"There's nothing to tell," I had said, pushing his jacket at him, urging him to leave. I had watched as he buckled his belt and put on his socks, far slower than I wanted him too.

I ignored the familiar hurt on his handsome face and knew that I shouldn't be so cruel, but I had been honest with him from the beginning. I didn't want a relationship or to fall in love. I just wanted someone to remind me that I didn't have to be alone, and I didn't want him to stay.

"How long are we going to keep doing this, Olivia? I want... more."

"I don't, Clay. Please." I didn't watch as his face darkened.

"If you gave me a chance, I could make you happy."

I didn't believe in happiness anymore.

I rubbed my eyes, exhausted as I silenced my phone, and tried not to think about the man who wanted far more from me than I was ever going to be willing to give him.

"You okay?" Danny's voice was rough and welcome in my ears. I turned to look at him as he drove, his eyes puffy and bloodshot, mirroring my own.

"I'm okay," I said, trying to mean it.

We drove the entire rest of the way in silence, each of us wrapped up in our own thoughts, our emotions heavy and thick. I stared out of the window into the darkness and prepared myself to walk into a silent home without Jill or Chase.

It was the moment I had been trying to imagine for a

long time, and now that it was in front of me, I wasn't sure if I could do it.

"I'm glad we did this together, Livvie," Danny said, breaking the silence. "I was worried that we couldn't, but this was good. It was good for Jill, and it was good for us."

I nodded, afraid that if I opened my mouth that tears would fall from my eyes.

"Yes," I managed to croak out. I tried to ignore how the sound of his voice still pulled at me from a place so deep inside that I had buried it and forgot that it existed.

I could tell he was smiling in the darkness.

"I've always regretted hurting you... leaving like I did. I hate myself every day for what I did to you and I'll never forgive myself. It was a shit way to end our life together..." Danny's voice had an edge to it that I'd never heard before. I tried to ignore the effect it had on me.

"That was a long time ago," I said trying not to think about the pain that his betrayal had caused. I had worked hard to own my part of our separation, though I had never told him about it. "I hurt you and you hurt me. We could point fingers at each other all night, but in the end, I refused to do things that would've made our lives better, and I left you alone."

He sighed as though an enormous weight had been lifted from his shoulders, and I knew that he deserved more than the guilt and shame that he had carried for so long.

He was alone now, too, and had been for a long time. The woman he'd left me for had been an escape from a sad life, and although he had dated many women on and off, he'd never found one that stuck.

"Are you going to be okay?" Danny's eyes were bright and luminescent in the reflection of the streetlights as he turned onto my street.

"Yes," I managed. He stopped the car and got out without looking in my direction. He walked over to my side and opened the door but was careful to keep his distance as I exited the car.

"I can stay for a bit... if you'd like," he offered. His voice halted as though he was afraid of every word as it was coming out of his mouth.

"No. Go ... home," I said. It had been a long day and I was drained. I knew that he must be, too, and even though he didn't have far to go, I wanted him to get home safely.

Danny paused as he turned to walk back around to the driver's side. "Call me if you need anything. Anything at all."

"I will," I said, knowing that I wouldn't call him even if I was on fire. I knew that I needed to leave him alone. He had suffered enough.

"Okay ... " he paused and turned, and for a split second I thought he might hug me. I braced for it, wanting him to but terrified that he would. I knew that if he touched me that I would beg him to stay, and I didn't want that to happen. There was a part of me that would always love him. Always want him. We were Danny and Liv, and it had taken me so many years to learn how to be someone without him.

Slowly, he turned back toward his car and opened his car door and got in without saying good-bye.

I walked toward the house and listened to his truck as it pulled away, forcing myself not to turn around. I knew that if I did, he would see that I was crumbling.

If he saw my face, he would know that I was sinking again, back into the darkness that refused to let me go.

CHAPTER EIGHT

Olivia, Age Forty-Five

SAYING goodbye to Jill was harder than I thought it would be, but not as difficult as not knowing where Chase was. I knew that I had nobody to blame but myself and with Jill off to college, I had even more time to think about and miss Chase more than ever.

He had been my baby before Jill was born. He came along right before the darkness began to consume me. I always wondered if things would've been different if we hadn't had Jill. The thought of it plagued me, filling me with guilt for even considering a life without Jill, but I realized that Chase had needed so much more.

More than I had ever given him.

Strangely enough, when I looked back I realize that the darkness had always been there but I had been able to ignore it until after the babies started coming. After Chase was born, the darkness came upon me unexpectedly.

With Ben and Chase, I was more exhausted than I ever

remembered, with both boys demanding so much, Ben's tiny face often pulling mine close. "More, Mommy. More!" Ben always wanted so much more than I was able to give, especially when Chase was born, and I couldn't remember the last time I had a good night's sleep. Chase's howls were imbedded in my brain with nothing comforting him, nothing giving either of us peace.

I desperately wanted to adore his sweet, cherubic face but his constant crying made me want to throw him at a wall. It was at those moments that I could feel my mother in me, and I knew that I didn't deserve to have such beautiful children, or any children at all for that matter.

God, how I hated myself.

"Mommy, Chase crying! Make him stop!" Ben would lay on the ground, covering his ears. I would have to leave Chase to cry in his crib, unable to soothe him, and afraid to touch him for fear I would hurt him.

Finally, on a Thursday, I had enough as I picked up the phone and dialed Allison for the first time of many, my fingers shaking uncontrollably as I attempted to punch the numbers several times. Just as I was about to give up, tears running down my cheeks, I pushed the last number and the phone was finally ringing.

When her voicemail came up, I cried out, lost as I nearly threw the phone to the ground.

"Please... I need help. Please call me," I cried before I hung up.

The next few moments felt like an eternity as I lay on the ground, Chase cried uncontrollably in the background with Ben screaming at me to get him. "Mommy, make him stop! Make him stop! Mommeeeeeee!"

I heard the phone ringing but I no longer cared. I no longer wanted to do anything but lay on the ground. I was paralyzed, unable to move or talk. I could barely force myself to breathe, my body exhausted. I could smell my breath pushing back at me from the hard floor and I wanted to gag. I didn't remember the last time I had showered or brushed my teeth, the boys sapping every bit of energy out of me. I could feel myself disappearing the longer I lay there until I could no longer hear them. I was a pile of nothingness, and for the first time in a long time, the anger and exhaustion fell away.

I knew that Ben was shaking me, but I couldn't feel it. I could feel nothing, and I was happy.

Happy in the nothingness.

That was the first time that I fell so far into the darkness, and didn't know if I would ever make my way back out, but thankfully I did, Allison saving me from myself.

She cleaned me up, rescued me, and began to help with the kids, all because I had asked her to. With her help, I came back to life and was finally able to be the mother I was supposed to be.

The second time I got lost in the darkness, Chase was five and he found me before anyone else did.

Chase and I walked to the end of the driveway in the morning like we usually did and waited for the bus. He turned around to wave right before he got on. He lingered for an extra moment and gave me the sweetest smile, melting my heart like he often did.

I turned slowly toward the house, savoring the sweetness of his heart as I looked forward to some rare time alone. Jill had spent the night with Danny's parents, and they were keeping her all day to give me some time to myself.

The day started out like it always did, but quickly began to unravel when the dishwasher started leaking in the middle of a cycle, emptying water all over the floor.

I had been trying to do more around the house, starting with the laundry. Danny had grown more distant than ever, barely even kissing me on his way out of the door in the morning. While the counseling helped, it was barely putting a dent into my larger issues, and we were existing as strangers.

He was growing more frustrated and impatient and couldn't understand why the dishes never got done or why dinner didn't get made. "You're home all day, Livvie. What do you do with yourself?"

He didn't understand that the days seemed to slip away, some faster and some slower, but no matter what I did nothing came together the way I had planned it out the night before. I'd promised at our last counseling session that I would try harder, so I made myself a list, and at the top was "Do the laundry".

I was lonely without him. He was my rock and my best friend, but he could barely even look at me anymore, and I knew that I only had myself to blame. I had tried and failed so many times to be a good mother and wife, but when it came down to it, I couldn't do it.

I wasn't good at anything, and I knew from the empty look in his beautiful eyes that Danny was finally giving up on me. It had taken far longer than I ever thought it would but as the end was becoming clearer, I realized how desperately I wanted to stop it. I didn't want him to surrender to his frustration with my mental illness. I didn't want him to walk away when there was still so much left to try.

But I realized that I'd asked for so much already, living on borrowed time and love that I hadn't earned.

The water flooding out of the machine dumping water all over the floor and all over me was overwhelming, and none of the usual calming techniques worked. Nothing I did could make me get to the place I needed to be as the panic welled up inside, more intense than the one before.

Soaked to the skin with soapy water, something broke inside, the tears coming down uncontrollably.

I saw myself as he must see me. Completely useless. Unable to even do laundry right.

Unable to do anything right.

I don't remember opening the bottle of pills and taking them all. I don't remember getting sleepier or feeling panic or regret. I don't even remember drinking down the remainder of a bottle of vodka that had been sitting untouched in the liquor cabinet for months.

Chase had gotten home from school, and while I usually met him at the bus at the end of our driveway, this day I didn't so the bus driver let him off. He knew that occasionally I overslept and didn't get up to meet him, and he always watched him until he got into the house.

The door was unlocked and Chase called out for me, but I didn't answer. After he'd grabbed a cookie, he wandered throughout the quiet house trying to find me.

"Mommy," he called anxiously, as he left the cookie on the nightstand in my bedroom, only half-eaten. "Mommy!"

I don't remember hearing him even though he said I looked him right in the eye. I only remember wishing that I could fade away faster from a world that I was clearly not meant to be in.

I thought I had the strength to navigate through it, but I realized with every failure that it was never going to happen.

I hadn't planned for Chase to find me.

I hadn't thought of anything else beyond the nothingness.

Dr. Sullivan told me years later that Chase suffered

post-traumatic stress disorder from finding me on the floor, half-conscious, unable to wake me completely. I'll never know the terror that went through him as he struggled to find the phone and dial 911 like we taught him, and even though he said he didn't remember, I couldn't see how it couldn't.

While it didn't affect him for many years afterward, despite therapy for him and for the rest of us, it didn't matter. The damage had been done, and nothing could ever undo the horror that had been planted inside of my youngest son.

Watching the nightmares that plagued him because he had to watch the paramedics try and revive me, was my penance. I would never forgive myself for what I had done to him.

But then he grew up, and I thought he might be safe because he seemed normal. Immune.

I thought that perhaps he had escaped the aftermath of a childhood with an unstable mother who loved him more than she could express and a father who had nothing else to give.

I was wrong.

Chase had hidden himself from all of us until he disappeared into a world of his own, pretending to be well-adjusted and normal. But then he met friends in college who introduced him to a world of drugs where he realized that he could hide from the painful memories and nightmares that haunted him when he was awake and asleep.

It was only then that I realized I was truly lost once again.

Lost from Danny, Chase, and finally, myself.

CHAPTER NINE

Olivia, Age Forty-Five

"YES, I know that I missed my appointment. Will you please just schedule another one?" I was exasperated, and Dr Sullivan's receptionist was such a bitch. She always had been.

"You know that I have to check with her first, Olivia. When you miss an appointment, she has to approve another one. This has always been the policy. Always." She emphasized the word always and I wanted to swear at her, but I didn't.

"I know. Please check with her and let me know." I knew I would have to go through this and should've prepared myself but I hadn't.

A week had gone by since Danny and I dropped Jill off at school, and I had barely gotten out of bed. A week had gone by since I'd last seen Danny or heard the sound of his voice. I felt the way I did when Danny had moved out, empty and alone.

Jill was doing well and loved college like I knew she would. I loved that with text messaging I could camouflage myself with emojis and exclamation points. Only Danny could tell that I wasn't handling it well, but neither was he. As well as he knew me, I knew him even better.

Even after he'd moved out, he saw or talked to Jill and the boys every day. Jill was his baby and not even our issues were going to keep him away from her.

"Are you okay?" Danny texted on Monday.

"No, are you?"

"No."

There was nothing left to say. Our lives were empty. No Ben. No Jill.

No Chase.

The phone rang and I jumped.

"Hello?"

"Dr Sullivan has an opening today at four o'clock. Can you be here then?"

I looked at the clock in my kitchen.

11:00.

"Yes. I can make it by then."

The receptionist hung up.

Bitch.

I searched the cabinets for the coffee and found it. I needed coffee. I needed more than coffee, but coffee would help.

I wondered what I would do to pass the time.

I thought back to the couples' therapy that Dr Sullivan had suggested for Danny and me after Chase found me in the bathtub. We had been taking Chase to therapy, and Dr Sullivan had strongly encouraged Danny and I to meet with someone, too. Danny had been skeptical, unsure that he wanted to sit down with a stranger and bare his soul. Dr

Sullivan sent us to a colleague in her practice that insisted we call him by his first name, Tom, because she couldn't be my therapist and our marriage counselor.

Tom was in his late forties, laid back, but matter-of-fact, and even though he didn't know us, he seemed to understand us immediately.

"So you're angry with Olivia?" he said to Danny after our first session and well into our second.

"Yes. I'm angry." Danny said, more forcefully than he ever had before. "I'm angry that she would let Chase see her like that. I'm angry that it's messed him up the way that it has. And I'm angry that she doesn't take her medication because according to her, she doesn't want to be sick."

The therapist looked at me and I crumbled under his gaze. I was used to Dr Sullivan, and she knew me. She knew that I wasn't a bad person and that I struggled, but this guy was more intense, and I wasn't sure that he was on my side.

"Is that true, Olivia? Do you not take your medication?" Tom asked, his hands folded, his gaze penetrating through me.

"I... uh... I forget. I mean, I don't want to *not* take it, but I forget. I really do keep thinking that I'm going to get better and that I won't need it anymore." I fought the urge to squirm in my seat.

"How long do you forget to take it for?" Tom was asking the same questions that Danny asked, and I wondered if he had told him to ask me that.

I sat still, my cheeks getting hot.

I didn't want to tell him that I would forget for weeks at a time. I didn't want to tell him I didn't forget but that I just hoped I wouldn't need it. I hoped that I would feel differently and that I wouldn't just spiral into the abyss which is what always seemed to happen. I didn't want to tell him that when I took all of the pills, I hadn't taken my medication for over a month and that I didn't even remember doing it.

I should've been hospitalized but I refused, even though I knew that Danny wanted me to be. But I had been taking my medication since then, even though it made me feel anxious and withdrawn, disinterested in Danny and in the world. Dr Sullivan had changed my meds over the years trying to find the right one, but it seemed as though we were constantly adjusting, and this time was no different.

I still didn't feel like myself, but nothing could compare to the pain my baby, my Chase, was going through. He had withdrawn into a world of his own, one that no longer involved me.

"I can tell by the look on your face that there are things you want to say to Olivia, Danny. Do you want to say them now?" Tom prodded Danny, and I wondered what he was trying to do.

The look on Danny's face frightened me. His eyes were dark, and he looked like a stranger, like someone I had never even met.

Danny took a deep breath. His face turned red, and he looked as though he might explode, the vein popping out of his forehead like it did when he was really angry.

"I'm pissed off, Livvie. I... I... can't even begin to tell you how angry I am that you would do something like this to our son. It's our child, Goddammit! Why would you do that to yourself knowing that he would come home and find you? Why would you do something so selfish?" The heat from his anger radiated toward me and I melted. He was seething, and I knew that he had been keeping his anger in for the sake of the kids, but in the cocoon of Tom's office, he felt safe to unleash it. "I never could've imagined that you would hurt our family this way. I thought you loved us more than that!"

"I'm sorry! I'm sorry, Danny. I don't... I don't want..." I tried to catch my breath but couldn't. I knew what I had done to my baby and to our family. I did love them, but I didn't want there to be something wrong with me. I just wanted to be normal, like I was when Danny and I first met. I didn't want to be this person who hurt her babies.

I hated this person that I had become.

The nightmares that Chase was having were proof of his pain. Every night he cried out, "Mom, wake up! Wake up! Why are you bleeding? Oh my goodness! Oh my goodness! Dad, help me! Mom, nooooo! Please wake up, oh God!"

Chase clung to me for dear life one moment and the next he was angry with me, and I couldn't blame him.

Our entire family had been thrown into a downward spiral, and there was no one to blame but me. Even Jill, who was only three at the time, suffered from the angry silence in the house, often hiding in her room for hours or reading alone, afraid to ask her big brothers to play. She was so quiet that there were times when I forgot she existed, always careful not to be disruptive.

"Olivia, do you think that you are sick?" Tom asked, pointedly but kind.

I'd sat and stared at my fingers for a long time. The nails were chewed to the quick, and my thumbs were torn up where I had ripped away the skin.

I hated my hands. They hurt and we're hideous to look at. I always hid them so people couldn't see what I did to them when I was anxious or upset. I was ashamed of them.

They were ugly.

Like my soul.

"Yes," I said, feeling Tom and Danny's eyes on me. I stared down at my hands, afraid to look up because I knew that I would cry and may never stop.

I heard Danny suck in his breath but he remained silent.

"What do you think you can do about it?" Tom asked, his voice low and soothing as though he were talking to a frightened child.

"Nothing. I can't do anything about it, Tom. There's something inside of my brain that isn't right, and no matter what I do or what I take, I can't make it right. This is in my blood and my bones. I'm just fucked, and there is absolutely nothing I can do about it."

OLIVIA, Age Seven

ROGER HAD MOVED in to the tiny trailer, and the space seemed to close in tight to an uncomfortable size.

Olivia hid as much as she could so that she didn't have to be near him, especially when Mommy was away. He was big and gross and when he smiled at her, it was as though he wanted to reach inside and steal her soul.

She wanted to tell Molly, but Molly was like a walking zombie who barely spoke or looked at anyone. She barely came out of their room, and when she did, all she did was watch television, completely unaware of anything around her.

Mommy didn't notice anything wrong with Roger at all, and if she did, she didn't seem to care.

At night, Olivia could hear sounds coming from Mommy's room, and in the morning, Roger grinned at her with brown teeth that made the hair on Olivia's neck stand up. Mommy kept trying to get her to kiss him good-night, but she refused, running outside every time she tried to make her. She knew that she wouldn't be able to get away with it too much longer because Mommy was becoming more persistent.

"He's your new daddy now, Olivia, so you need to treat him with some respect."

Weeks went by, and Molly finally began to speak. The sound of her voice made Olivia happier than she could ever remember being before but she was careful not to seem too eager. At times she felt like she was approaching a stray dog that she wanted to pet, and she spoke gently so she wouldn't scare her away.

"Are you feeling better?" Olivia asked, her voice soft as she approached her outside the trailer at the picnic table where they ate breakfast.

"Yes," Molly said, attempting a smile.

Olivia tried not to stare at her sister. She was afraid if she did, Molly would see how alarmed she was at how badly she looked. Still scraggly, her clothes hung on her as though they belonged to a stranger that was two sizes larger than her. Her hair hung dull and lifeless down her back, and her bright eyes appeared to be washed out. But Olivia thought she was still pretty. Sunshine will help. Olivia knew that if she could just get Molly outside in the sun that she might get back to her old self again.

Molly picked at her cereal and took tiny bites. She chewed as though it hurt, and Olivia had the urge to take her food and feed her.

Olivia sat in silence, just happy to be near her in the bright morning light. This was one of the first times Molly had been outside, and Olivia didn't want to spoil it.

Molly suddenly looked at Olivia, her eyes wide.

"My baby..." she said, tears filling her eyes.

Olivia moved closer and threw her arms around Molly.

"It died, Livvie." Tears fell down Molly's cheeks and she didn't move to wipe them away. "She killed my baby."

Olivia thought about the blood and shuddered, a bitter taste in her mouth. She knew that Molly had to be right. There couldn't have been that much blood unless it was true.

"Where were you for so long?" Olivia asked carefully.

"She put me in the psych ward of the hospital and then made Vince's mom come and get me. I stayed with them for a while, but then Vince's new girlfriend didn't want me there anymore, and his mom threatened to call Children's Services and the police if she didn't pick me up. They were already asking questions at the hospital, and that bitch didn't want to raise anymore red flags, so she came and got me even though she didn't want to."

It was the most Molly had spoken to her in months, and Olivia listened intently.

"I'm sorry that I left you Livvie-Lou. I didn't want to. I swear." Molly put her hand on Olivia's arm and pulled her close. "I promise, I would never have left you alone with that monster if I didn't have a choice."

Molly sobbed into Olivia's shoulder as the sisters held tightly to one another.

Olivia was relieved to know that Molly would never have left her.

"I know, Molly," Olivia cried into her shoulder. "I missed you so much. Please, don't ever leave me again."

Molly held her by the shoulders and looked her in the eye.

"I swear, Lu. I'll never leave you again. I'll protect you

always! I promise." Olivia held on tight, her heart full of sadness and promise. She'd never felt so full of sorrow, yet safe at the same time. She cried for Molly's unborn baby that Mommy had killed, but she was happy that Molly was finally home and herself once more.

"You have to promise me one thing, Lu," Molly said, pulling away. Her voice was serious, and Olivia knew that what she was about to say was important.

"No matter what happens or where I am, under no circumstances are you to ever be alone with Roger. I've tried to tell that bitch to protect you but she won't listen. I was going to call the police, but the landline is dead because she can't pay the bill, so I'm going to the police about it later today. I've been keeping a close eye on you, but stay away from him. Do you promise?"

Olivia nodded, her eyes large.

Molly's tone scared her. Even though Molly didn't say why she needed to stay away from him, she could tell by the sound of her voice that it was important. Deep down she knew she should keep her distance from him and Molly confirmed it.

"I'll protect you. I promise." Molly kissed her on the forehead and held her tight. Olivia knew that there was nobody who loved her more in the entire world than her sister. "I'll make sure nobody ever hurts you. I'm so sorry I left you but I swear, it'll never happen again."

Olivia squeezed Molly tight. She never wanted to let go of her again and wondered how she had made it so long without her.

Molly was everything to her, and she couldn't imagine ever living in a world where she wasn't.

Ever.

CHAPTER TEN

Olivia, Age Forty-Five

A FEW WEEKS after Jill went to school and I was finally able to get in to see Dr Sullivan, I started to feel normal.

At least normal for me.

I had graduated to leaving the house a few times a week and showering on a more consistent basis.

I no longer felt like I was lying to Jill when she asked how I was and I told her that I was doing well with the happy faced emoji. We rarely had verbal conversations but texted about twenty times a day, and I accepted that it was the only way I would be able to stay in touch with her regularly.

But one day without warning, I was knocked down flat.

I reluctantly opened my eyes as the sun came up, and the alert on my phone said "Chase's birthday."

My heart sank so far that and I thought I might implode. I wondered if Danny would remember, and instantly I knew that he would. He was a great parent and would never forget his child's birthday. Unlike me, which is why my phone had to alert me and not my heart, like Danny's would.

The tears were instant, and I wondered for the thousandth time where Chase was and what he was doing. I picked up my phone and texted him like I had done so many times before, praying this time he might answer.

"Good morning, baby. I don't know if you'll get this but if you do, happy birthday. We all love and miss you. Please call me. Please come home soon."

I stared at the phone, unblinking, like I always did when I sent him a text. I held my breath waiting for him to respond.

One minute. Two minutes. Twenty minutes went by with nothing. I had been staring at the phone for twenty minutes, unmoving.

I could hardly blame him for ignoring me. I understood what I had done to him and how I had scarred him, permanently. I'd had well over a decade to think about it.

It had been exactly eight months and five days since I had seen him last.

He had come home from college for the weekend, and I knew the moment I laid eyes on him that there was something wrong. His usually lanky frame was frighteningly thin, and his beautifully bright skin was sallow and almost gray. I reached for him the moment he came through the door, but he pulled away.

"Hi, Mom," he'd mumbled.

"Hi, Kiddo," I said, pretending as though him pulling away from me didn't hurt like hell. "How've you been?"

"Fine," he said, refusing to look me in the eye. How long had it been since we'd talked, really talked?

When he was a boy, he talked to me all of the time and I listened.

I hung onto his every word as though he was the most important thing in the world. I had done the same with Ben, both boys talking to me about every thought that came into their minds; their favorite baseball player, why French fries from one fast food restaurant were better than those from another, why boys were always better than girls, and how much they preferred dogs over cats.

They told me everything, even the things they were embarrassed to talk about, and I relished every word. Even when I wasn't well, I still tried to listen because the sound of their little voices gave me hope. Sometimes it was the only thing that got me through the day.

Even after Chase found me in the bathtub, he still talked to me. He was young, and even though he forgave me, the fearful look in his eyes and the way he clung to me let me know that he was terrified of losing me.

His fear changed him forever, and as he grew older, it turned to anger and then resentment.

In his teens he temporarily rebelled by drinking and smoking marijuana, but he was an excellent student and got into college with ease. Danny and Ben set him straight and he went onto college and did well for the first half of the year. But suddenly, I watched as the darkness began to consume him, too.

I realized with shock and certainty that he reminded me of Molly, the recognition of her in him paralyzing me.

More and more, Chase began to pull away, the silence between us unbearable as he avoided me at all costs. He only came back home the last weekend I saw him because he needed to do laundry and pick up things he'd forgotten during Christmas break. I'd seen him a few weeks before but I hadn't remembered him looking so bad.

"Are you sick, Chase?" I'd asked, reaching for him to feel his forehead.

"Dammit, Mom, I'm fine. Stop nagging!" He had stomped off to his room liked he'd done when he was five, angry with me as always.

He went to Danny's house to spend most of his time, refusing to be alone with me even for a moment.

"Are you okay?" Danny texted, knowing that Chase's rejection would consume me.

"No, but it doesn't matter. Watch him, Danny. He's not okay."

"I will," Danny responded.

That was the last time Chase had been home, and it was the last time we knew where we was.

The only message that he sent was to Danny.

"Dad-I'm dropping out of school. It's not for me. I need to get away, escape. I can't do this anymore with Mom and need to be away. I'm sorry."

The police searched but didn't find anything. There was no cell phone signal and no sign of him anywhere. His good friends told us that he took off with a girl he had told them about but that they never met; an addict.

They told us that he was lost.

We waited, our entire family traumatized by our loss, feeling Chase's absence collectively but painfully alone.

I thought about Chase's fourth birthday when I picked out the bright red fire truck that had fascinated him in the store the week before. Ben had gone with me to pick it out.

"Chase will like that one, Mom." Ben had said, his dark brown eyes glinting with excitement.

"Do you think so?" I asked, proud of myself for remembering how much he had liked it.

"Yes!" Ben's voice was full of excitement and a touch of jealousy.

When Chase opened it, his face was a beautiful mix of awe and happiness. "I love it, Mommy!" He squealed as he ran to me and hugged me as hard as he could, a ball of sheer energy.

I wondered if he remembered the happiness of that day and how much he loved his shiny red fire truck. I wondered where he was and what he was doing.

Did he even realize it was his birthday? Was he with someone he loved or loved him?

I wondered if he ever thought about me and how much I loved him.

"You don't love me," he'd said to me when he was fifteen.

"Of course I love you, Chase!" I told him that I loved him every day. He had saved me from myself, and I owed him my life. "I've always loved you, ever since the moment I knew that I was pregnant with you!"

"Did you love me when you were trying to kill yourself? You knew I would find you! You meant to end it all and leave us! You were being selfish!" His anger had been palpable and building for months.

At fifteen he towered over me, the darkness so evident even then.

"If you loved me, you wouldn't have tried to leave me," his voice caught as he said it and my heart cracked.

Shame flooded over me.

"I'm sorry, baby. I'm sorry. I can't say it enough. I can't ever take it back but I'm sorry for what I've done to you." My words felt empty in my mouth. I had betrayed the ones I loved the most, and even though there were some things I couldn't control, I had still made choices that had cut them deep.

My apology felt insignificant compared to the pain I had caused, and every time I said I was sorry, helplessness welled up within. It suffocated me in the futility of my words. Nothing I could ever say or do could turn back time and change what I'd done.

I'd scarred him forever, and it was unforgivable and self-ish. I hated myself for what I'd done.

The self-loathing came in waves, and I no longer tried to protect myself from it.

As I hoped for Chase to respond to my text, I knew deep down that he wouldn't.

He was as lost as I was, spiraling down a hopeless abyss, sent there by the person who was supposed to love and protect him the most.

I knew that nothing I would ever do could ever make up for what I'd done.

I would never deserve forgiveness for destroying my sweet son.

Olivia, Age Forty-Five

I FELL asleep on my bed with my phone in my hand.

I was dreaming of a familiar song, it was mine and Danny's song. The song we'd fallen in love to. The song they'd played at our wedding.

I woke up with a start as I realized that the song was my phone ringing. It was Danny's ringtone.

My heart was racing as his voice came through, loud and trembling. "Olivia, they think they've found him."

There was a sense of finality and no hope behind his words.

"What does that mean?" I asked as I sat up and tried to shake the blanket of sleep from my head. "Where did they find him? Is he alive? Is he okay?"

"I... he's not okay, Liv. Let me come and get you. I don't want to talk to you about it on the phone." Danny's voice was flat.

"No... tell me now, please." I begged.

"I'll be there in ten." Danny hung up not giving me a chance to say anything else.

I jumped out of bed and ran into the bathroom to brush my teeth. I smoothed my hair as best as I could, and wiped the crust from my eyes as I brushed furiously.

I smoothed on deodorant and was waiting on the front porch within five minutes, the blood pumping in my ears as I watched anxiously for Danny's truck to come around the corner.

As soon as I saw it I jumped up, and he'd barely stopped when I'd flung the door open.

"What is happening? Who called you?" The words were tumbling out of my mouth as he stared at me, his eyes red.

"Joe," Danny croaked out.

Joe had been his best friend in middle school. A police sergeant for Happy Endings, Danny had found him by accident when we'd begun searching for Chase.

"Where did they find him?" I asked, terrified of the answer.

"They think they found him in an abandoned building. His ID was there..." Danny spoke slowly as though he didn't want the words to come out.

"Who was he with? Is he okay?" I was desperate for answers, and Danny wasn't giving them quickly enough.

Danny turned and grabbed my hand, squeezing it tight, the look on his face made my heart stop.

"It's not good news, Liv. They think he overdosed."

I could barely hear him. His voice was so low that my good ear hardly registered his words.

"What does that mean?" I asked, every nerve ending suddenly on high alert. "Is he okay? Is he in the hospital?"

Danny suddenly pulled me close, crushing me against his chest, his voice quivering as he cried. "He's gone, Liv. He's gone."

His words echoed in my ears, and my heart stopped. Time stopped instantly.

Danny released me as he pulled away.

He searched my face for a reaction but there was none.

"Liv, did you hear what I said?" Danny put his hands on my shoulders. He was squeezing me but I didn't care.

"Yes. I heard you," I pushed him away forcefully. "Where are you taking me?"

His eyes widened in surprise at my response. I always fell apart into a puddle of sadness and hysteria when things began to fall apart. Danny's words didn't seem real to me, and I couldn't grasp the thought that my boy could be gone forever.

"I have to go and identify the body to make sure it's him. Joe said he matched the description and that they found his wallet. The ... body has started to decompose but ..."

"Let's go then," I said, not recognizing my own voice.

Danny turned and carefully put the car in gear and pulled away, wiping his eyes with the back of his sleeve.

I stared out of the window for the entire forty-five

minute drive trying to feel something. The numbness terrified me in a way that nothing ever had.

Even during the darkest moments, I'd always been able to feel something. Feeling nothing would mean that I was finally dead but still breathing, and I wasn't sure if I could survive that.

The car slowed and Danny pulled into a parking spot in an empty and dark parking lot next to a cold brick building.

"We're here," he said, searching my face for a response.

I took a deep breath.

"It's not going to be him," I said, my voice flat.

"Liv... " Danny's eyes were pleading.

"It's not going to be him," I repeated.

"If it is... " He spoke slowly, choosing his words carefully, "I'll be with you. I promise, I'll be right there with you."

I stared through him, not wanting to hear his voice any longer. We sat in silence for a moment, soaking in the magnitude of what we were about to do.

"Are you ready?" I asked, placing my hand on his arm.

"No, but we don't have a choice." Danny grabbed the handle to open the door.

We walked in slowly. Joe was waiting for us, his dark eyes sympathetic.

"You're going to be meeting with the Medical Examiner, and he's going to show you some photographs. You'll have to confirm if the pictures are your son," he explained.

I kept my head down and refused to look at him. I didn't want to see the pity in his eyes.

The next hour was a blur as they ushered us into a comfortable but plain room with a soft leather couch.

"Do you want coffee, Olivia?" Joe asked as though he was afraid I would answer.

I shook my head.

The Medical Examiner came in and introduced himself. He was a small man with smooth skin and dark rimmed glasses. He squinted when he spoke as though he was concentrating on his words, his speech fast and his voice low. I struggled to hear him with my good ear, but he continued to speak, unaware that I wasn't following. Danny listened intently next to me, taking deep breaths and fighting back the tears that shined in his eyes.

We sat close on the couch and he held me against him. We hadn't been that close in a long time, and I leaned into the warmth of his body.

"Are you ready?" Danny asked me, his voice breaking into the Medical Examiner's garble.

I nodded but I wasn't ready. I would never be ready to face the possible death of my son.

For the first time I noticed the pictures that were face down on the table in front of us. The Medical Examiner had his hand protectively on top of them as if he was afraid they would turn over on their own.

As if in slow motion, his light brown hand turned the pictures over, one by one, and my breath caught.

The face in the pictures was grossly emaciated, his skin gray.

I imagined that the face had once been handsome and lively and now there was nothing but a shell left. The skin was stretched tightly over the bones, and there were dark puncture marks on the arms where needles had punched through the skin.

His dark hair looked dirty as though it hadn't been brushed in a very long time, and the teeth were black.

The cause of death wasn't evident, but I imagined that

the neglect and abuse heaped on his poor body had played a part of his demise.

I desperately searched the boy's face for any sign of familiarity. I had looked into Chase's face every day for his entire life and had memorized every feature, every line.

I could tell by the way he furrowed his brow when he was tired or irritated with me. I knew by the shade of blue in his eyes when he was happy or frustrated or ornery. I had sat for hours staring at him as a baby, and my fingertips could outline the shape of his face in my sleep.

I had been the worst mother, but that didn't stop me from loving him with everything inside of me. I had hurt him, but my heart could recognize him from a thousand miles away.

"It isn't him!" I said, suddenly.

Danny had been studying the pictures, staring at them as though the boy would wake up and tell him who he was.

"Liv..."

"It's not him!" The certainty in my voice surprised me.

"How do you know?" Danny asked looking lost.

"The freckle... on his temple... it's not there..." I pointed to the blank temple on the boy in the picture.

Danny look d dumbfounded. "You're right... Livvie, thank God, you're right."

I let go of the breath I had been holding in since we'd walked into the room.

"It's not him," Danny said, letting go of the tears he'd been holding back. "He has a dark brown freckle on his temple that was the spot Livvie used to kiss on him every day, ten times a day. She used to tell him that it was the spot God gave her to aim for whenever she wanted to kiss him. It's not on this boy... it's not him."

Memories flooded over me of kissing Chase on that very spot countless times.

Danny grabbed me and held me so tight I could barely breathe, but I didn't care. It was as though the room suddenly emptied of air, and as the tears began to flow, I realized that I might not be able to stop them. Everything I had been holding inside spilled out in an uncontrollable torrent of tears.

I could hear the Medical Examiner's voice but didn't try and understand any of the words. I could see the motion of Danny's head moving up and down as he answered, but I could hear nothing else but the sound of my own crying.

"It's time to go, Livvie," Danny stood me up, and I leaned against him as he walked me to his car unsure if I could make it on my own. My legs felt heavy, my body exhausted.

As he opened the door for me and helped me in the car, his lips suddenly found mine.

I hadn't felt his lips on mine for so long, and I realized how completely empty I had been without him.

As our lips moved together, hungry and needing, I held on to the moment, never wanting it to end. For the first time, my heart was bursting with hope, and I held on to him as tightly as I could, and I knew that I could never let him go again.

CHAPTER ELEVEN

Olivia, Age Forty-Five

KNOWING that the dead boy wasn't Chase was exhilarating, yet heartbreaking at the same time. I wanted to be happy that the boy wasn't Chase, but I still didn't know where he was and wasn't sure that he wasn't dead.

As we pulled in front of my house, I could tell that Danny was completely drained.

"Do you want to come in for coffee?" I asked, hesitantly.

"Sure," he said, no expression on his face. I couldn't remember ever seeing Danny this empty since the weeks after Chase disappeared.

We walked to the house in silence, and as I unlocked the door, I heard Danny say under his breath, "God, I miss this house."

I turned to face him, pained immediately by the anguish on his face. "I'm sorry."

"It's not your fault, Livvie." Danny sighed as he followed close behind me. His presence immediately filled the house, chasing away the emptiness that had been suffocating me for months.

"Do you want coffee or tea? I usually do tea this late at night."

He shrugged and I busied myself with making the tea while he wandered aimlessly through the rooms that he used to walk through every day. I watched him out of the corner of my eye marveling at how he seemed so at ease. It was as though he had never even left, and my heart ached at how much time had slipped away and forgotten all about us.

Tears threatened my eyes as I pushed them back, desperate for Danny not to see.

The kettle whistled, startling me as I wiped furiously at my face and took a deep breath.

"The house looks good, Liv," Danny said, his appreciation warming me.

"Thank you," I was afraid to make eye contact for fear that he would see straight through me.

He had a way of always knowing my inner thoughts. I didn't want him to see how much it wrecked me to know that within a short time, he would be leaving again, with no reason to come back. I knew that I would have to face the emptiness of a home that was no longer full of chaos and laughter. As imperfect as it had all been, there had been love.

Always love.

With Chase, Ben, and Jill gone, the crushing loneliness became more unbearable with every passing day. I dreaded the moment Danny would be gone, too.

As the tea steeped, Danny finally settled into the space at the table that used to be his.

The silence between us was comforting, neither of us needing to talk. Even though we hadn't spent much time together in a couple of years, after the night we'd had, it was as though no time had gone by.

I'd spent most of my life with him and he was familiar, his presence calming. I longed for the days when he had been my Danny and I had been his Livvie, and moments like this made me realize how much I still missed him every day.

I handed him his cup and watched as he sipped it carefully. I sat across from him, aching from the familiarity of it all.

"Feeling better?" I asked, not really wanting to break the silence but concerned by the tired lines around his eyes.

"Yes," he nodded. "Thank you for the tea."

"Of course," I smiled as I fought the urge to reach across the table and grab his hands.

He stood up abruptly and my heart dropped.

It was already late, and he would be leaving any moment. He leaned against the counter and rubbed his face trying to shake off the exhaustion. Even as tired as he was, he still looked as handsome as ever, and my heart longed for him.

I tried not to think about how much he looked as though he still belonged here.

"I can't believe this is happening," I said as I stood up, steeling myself for his inevitable departure. "I can't believe Chase hasn't come home."

"I know, Livvie. What in the hell is he doing? Where is he?" Danny asked, frustrated.

"God, I wish I knew!" I thought about the poor boy in the pictures and shuddered. I prayed that Chase wouldn't end up like him, emaciated and alone, dying alone. "He just can't be... he can't be..."

Danny put his arm around me and looked me in the eye.

"Don't lose hope, Livvie. He'll come home. You can't give up."

"It's been eight months, Danny. Where is he? What if... he's..."

"No. Stop..." Suddenly Danny's lips were on mine, soft and warm, and I melted into him. I still dreamt of moments like these as much as I tried not to. I had tried desperately to push him out of my mind, but he was a part of me, and nothing could rid myself of his memory.

I was barely breathing without him.

As he kissed me, it became even clearer how much I needed him. I suddenly felt stronger and more alive.

"Stop talking, Livvie," Danny murmured, his eyes closed. That was his answer whenever he felt as though I was talking too much. He distracted me with his lips, which always worked.

He pulled away, his lips lingering near mine, and I could feel his breath on my face. I missed being this close to him and yearned for it every day. Even when he was gone I thought of it. Thought of him.

"Don't you ever think about him? Don't you wonder?" I murmured.

"Yes, Livvie. Of course I do! Every day. Every minute of every day. Dammit!" Danny said as he took a step back. "Of course I wonder! I always wonder! When I'm not missing you and Jill, I'm worried about Ben or I'm thinking about Chase! You are my entire world, and nothing makes sense without all of you! Nothing!"

"But you're the one who filed for divorce!" I ached inside, wondering if his words were real. "You wanted out, and I can't blame you."

"No, Livvie. I didn't want out. I was just ... stuck. I didn't know what to do anymore and out seemed like the only direction to go. I had tried everything else." He leaned his forehead against mine and sighed, all of the heaviness he has been carrying flooding out all at once. "We've been through this all before. Love isn't the issue."

Love had never been the issue. My rages, the uncontrollable anger, the ups and the downs and the unpredictability of it all had been the issue. When the medication was controlled and things would even out, I convinced myself that I was better and stopped taking it, or cut back, or forgot to pick it up. The cycle had been constant, and each time, the fall out eroded our relationship a little at a time until there was nothing left.

"I'm sorry that I never gave you another option other than out. I'm sorry for a lot of things that I did and so many things I didn't. I was a terrible wife... and mother." I said, the words tumbling out.

"It wasn't all your fault, Livvie. We've just had far more than two people should ever have to deal with. When is it just too damned much?" Danny asked the question we often wondered to ourselves but rarely said out loud.

"I'm just so relieved that boy wasn't Chase, but I so sorry for his mother who doesn't know he's gone yet," I said, wiping the tears from my eyes.

Even though I had been fighting it, they had been flowing intermittently and I couldn't stop them, nor did I want to. Being sober made me feel everything, and I realized why I'd once turned to alcohol to numb the pain.

As I thought about that boy who had resembled Chase dying alone, it broke my heart. Being alone was the worst feeling of all, but I didn't feel that when I was with Danny. I welcomed everything that he made me feel, the wonderful and the awful, but in the end I knew that I was alone, which felt worse than death.

"I feel terrible for whoever that poor boy was, but thank God it wasn't my baby."

"I feel the same," Danny said, pulling me toward him by my belt loops, my thighs leaning on his legs. Being this close made me dizzy, my body waking up in ways that reminded me of how dead I had been inside.

He leaned his forehead against mine like he used to, and I felt that familiar longing for the Danny that used to love me more than anything. I held my breath, afraid to move, terrified that if I did I would wake up and find that this was all a dream.

Time froze as we stood together, absorbing one another, separated only by our clothing and the distance that had grown between us.

I could feel the space between us slowly closing the longer we held one another, and I never wanted the moment to end. It had been so long since I had felt this connected to anyone, and I had forgotten how it felt to want so much.

I barely felt it as Danny began to undress me, lost in the feel of his lips on my neck and his hands in my hair.

"Wait," I said, my brain jolting my body to a stop.

"What?" he asked, his teeth grazing my skin, making it difficult for me to think.

"What about your... uh... girlfriend?"

Danny paused for a moment, but then proceeded to unbutton my jeans and slide them down my hips.

"Do you want to talk about this now?" he murmured, his voice in my ear sending shivers down my spine.

"Y-y-yes," I said with much difficulty, electricity coursing through me everywhere his fingers touched.

"There was never anyone else for me... I've been on my own now for a long time. I just got lost..." Danny said, kissing my neck as I felt his fingers grazing my thighs. "There's only ever been you, Livvie. Ever."

I kissed him hungrily, peeling off his jeans and unbuttoning his shirt, enjoying the way that we still moved together in unison. It had been far too long since I had last touched his skin, and he responded immediately to my touch as though he had been waiting for it.

We kissed one another hungrily, our mouths coming together eager and desperate. I suddenly remembered how I had loved to kiss those lips, and how delicious he had always tasted. I had never kissed anyone else and had never desired anyone as much as I longed for him.

When we were finally naked, our bodies fell together in a messy tangle of arms and legs, our skin soft and sleek against each other.

We were as perfect as we had always been, remembering exactly what we needed from one another. Our breath came fast as we panted in unison, marveling at how we fit together like a beautifully broken piece of art, glued together with our love and passion. And when we finally lay against the pillows, clutching onto one another trying to catch our breath, I was complete for the first time in years.

And I knew that I was never going to push him away ever again.

CHAPTER TWELVE

Olivia, Age Seven

MOLLY HAD BEEN HOME for months, protecting Olivia from any chance that she might be alone with Roger.

Mommy couldn't understand why Olivia refused to acknowledge Roger or let Molly be alone in the room with him.

"You need to be nicer to Roger! If you don't fuck this up for me, he'll be your new daddy, you ungrateful slug," Mommy hissed at Molly.

"You're despicable! How can you not see that he's dangerous! He's not here for you. He's here for Olivia. Haven't you seen the creepy way he stares at her? Don't you pay attention to anything?" Molly whispered angrily, spitting the words at her.

"Don't be vile." The look in Mommy's eyes was hard, and Olivia could feel the shift in the air that told her she was walking on dangerous ground. "You're just jealous that I have someone and you don't. Well it's not my fault that you couldn't hold onto your boyfriend once you let him touch you. That's what you get for being a whore."

Molly sucked in her breath.

She'd tried to ignore how much Mommy's words hurt her, but no matter how hard she tried to make her heart, they still struck her to the core.

"If you don't get rid of him, you're going to be sorry!" Molly warned, pulling herself up tall until she towered over her mother. She'd been taller than her for some time, but had only just realized it. She knew she'd have to protect Olivia, and she had to do it at all costs.

"Are you threatening me?" Mommy asked, her eyes glittering sharply.

Molly stared at Mommy, her feet planted firmly where she stood. "I'm telling you... don't let him near her or you'll both be very sorry."

The door to the bathroom opened and a putrid smell wafted in the air. His shirt was greasy from days of wear, and he had three-day old stubble on his face. Ever since he'd been fired from his job, he never seemed to leave, and any space he occupied made the rest of the trailer seem so small.

Molly found it impossible to breathe normally when he was around, her disgust for him choking her.

"What's going on over there, kid?" The edge in his voice sent shivers down Molly's spine.

"N-n-n-nothing..." Molly stuttered.

"Tell him," Mommy's dared her.

Molly shook her head. "It was nothing," she muttered, suddenly feeling small.

"Are you sure about that? You look guilty as hell. Are you talking shit about me?" He stepped closer to her, his dark eyes burning a hole in hers. "Your mother told me that that I could do whatever I wanted to you. She said that I'm in charge here now, so if you got something to say to me, then say it or shut the hell up."

Molly closed her mouth and shook her head.

"That's what I thought." Roger said, his eyes never leaving her face. "I didn't think you'd have the guts to say it to my face."

Molly turned and walked out of the trailer, letting the door slam behind her as she did so.

Her heart was racing in her chest, and she knew without a doubt that Roger was dangerous to her and Olivia. She was terrified but there was no choice. She'd promised Olivia, and she wasn't going to let her down like her mother had done to her.

She knew that no matter what, she would have to protect them both at all costs.

CHAPTER THIRTEEN

Olivia, Age Forty-Six

MONTHS WENT by with no more leads.

I'd had yet another birthday. Ben and Jill were doing well in school, only coming home to do laundry or check in on me. They were happy to find that Danny and I were carefully finding our way back to one another, even though they both expressed caution. They'd seen the joy we gave one another, but had also witnessed the turmoil and explosiveness, sometimes caught in the middle.

"We just want you and dad to be happy, whether it's together or apart," Ben had said, wise beyond his years as he'd always been.

Danny and I decided to try couples therapy once again, with better results.

The anger and resentment we'd once carried for one another had lessened over our many years apart replaced by the excitement and exhilaration of rediscovering one another.

Our joint effort in finding Chase unified us even more as our search efforts were doubled, and we were able to discover a network of people who were committed to helping us find him.

We finally had a break when Danny received a phone call from a long lost friend. His cousin, Elizabeth, was a nurse at the hospital in Happy Endings and let him know about a patient that matched Chase's description. She'd lost her oldest son to a heroin overdose a few years before and had been on the lookout for Chase since he'd disappeared.

I was terrified.

I knew there had to be so many boys with Chase's blue eyes and brown hair and didn't want to get my hopes up.

Danny and I drove to Happy Endings, both of us on edge.

The town hadn't changed much over the years, the familiar landscape bringing back so many memories of a childhood and young life spent in misery. I hated the sight of it and had made it a point to never visit the small town. Yet as much as I hated to admit it, it felt like home.

It made me think of Molly, a sudden sadness coming over me.

The hospital was as small and quiet as the town, and needed to be updated. The paint on the walls needed to be retouched, and the decor looked tired and old like the place I had grown up in. I had promised myself that I would never go back, but I didn't have a choice. I would go anywhere to find Chase.

We walked in anxiously and went to the third floor to meet Elizabeth.

An older woman with bright red hair and a smattering of freckles across her nose met us as we got off the elevator.

Danny gave her a warm hug, lifting her tiny frame

easily off the ground as he did so.

I had only met her once at our wedding, but she reached over to pull me into a hug. The strength of her arms surprised me, and when she finally released me, I could see the pain in her hazel eyes. We'd connected on social media years before, but I never posted much, unable to see how posting pictures of my life when it was imploding could possibly help me or my family. I wanted desperately for us to be like the rest of the world, posting pictures of vacations and the first day of school, but knew that it would all be a lie, and it was one more fabrication that I couldn't bear to keep up.

Danny grabbed my hand and we held on to each other for dear life.

"I didn't want to get your hopes up, but when they brought this boy in last night, he fit Chase's description perfectly. I hadn't seen any pictures of him since he was about five, so it was difficult for me to tell if it was him, but I could see where there might be a resemblance. From what I've been able to get out of him, I thought it was possible that it could be him." Her voice was low as though she was sharing a secret. "I'm not supposed to share this kind of information, and I could lose my job, but if someone had helped me find my Joshua…"

Her bright eyes immediately filled with tears and she quickly blinked them back.

"Where did they find him?" I asked, my voice breaking.

"He was found alone, in an abandoned car, unconscious and nearly dead. They brought him in as an overdose case after reviving him with several shots of Narcan. The paramedics nearly lost him a couple of times but they were able to stabilize him, and he's been doing better for the past couple of hours."

"Is he awake?" Danny ran his fingers through his hair, the look in his eyes desperate.

"Barely," Elizabeth said. "It's going to take some time for him to get back to normal, but he's stable and looks like he'll pull through."

"What does that mean, exactly?" I asked, anxiously.

"He's going to live, but he's not aware of much. This boy, whoever he is, is going to need a lot of support and therapy if he's going to survive long-term. It's difficult to tell how he is physically until we are able to do a full work-up on him, but these cases only have a chance at a happy ending if they have a lot of love and support at home. If this is your Chase, he's in pretty bad shape." Elizabeth squeezed my hand and pulled me close as though preparing me for the moments ahead.

I was terrified.

What if we'd prepared for this and it wasn't him? What if it was him and he died just as we'd found him again? The questions were unbearable, and my hands began to shake.

Elizabeth held my hand tight as we walked toward the room, and as she opened the door, my heart dropped to my stomach.

Danny's sharp intake of breath let me know that he saw what I did.

Our Chase lay motionless in the bed, his skin a sickening gray. Even though he'd lost about thirty pounds since we'd seen him last, I would've recognized him anywhere.

Danny rushed over to the bed and pulled me with him.

I wanted to touch him but I was terrified. His eyes were closed, his long lashes lay soft against his cheek, and I was reminded of the many hours I would watch him sleep as a new baby. I wanted desperately to run my thumb over the dark freckle on his temple and kiss him on the head, but I hesitated, afraid to wake him.

Tears pricked my eyes as I sat on the side of his bed and picked up his hand and placed it in mine.

"It's Mom," I whispered. "Mom and Dad are here, Chase."

I could feel Danny's silent sobs as he stood against me. I put my arm around his waist and buried my head into him, breaking apart from the pain and the relief that we had finally found our boy.

Elizabeth stood nearby, her eyes glistening. "I'll leave you alone."

Chase continued to lay perfectly still, his body so alarmingly thin. I'd never seen him so thin in his entire life and it broke my heart. But he was alive, and that was all that mattered. After so long searching for our boy, he was finally here.

After an hour, Danny stepped out of the room to call Jill and Ben. He couldn't keep it from them any longer and knew they would be desperate to come home immediately.

I sat staring at Chase, afraid to move or breathe. I was terrified that if he woke up and saw me that he would immediately run from the room. The guilt overwhelmed me as I looked at my son and what I had done to him.

He'd missed out on a lot of normal things, and while Danny had provided the stability he'd needed, I had struggled in my sobriety and treatment and he'd paid the price.

I didn't deserve his forgiveness but I knew I had to try. I had to do everything in my power to show him that I could do the right thing and be the mother he needed, in spite of all of the things I had failed at as his mother.

Silent tears streamed down my face as I sat staring at the boy who had once loved touching my face while he cuddled in my lap. It hadn't all been bad, all of the memories bundled together like a ball of string, impossible to unravel without them hopelessly twisting together. I'd wanted to be the perfect mother, but I'd convinced myself that I didn't know how.

My mother, Cynthia, and my father, Lou, had been the worst parents in every possible way. Yet, a part of me had loved them and wanted their approval.

The only love I'd ever known and could remember was Molly, but they had tainted her for me, convincing me that she'd tried to kill me. I knew that none of that was an excuse for hurting my children, especially Chase, and that I needed to accept responsibility for what I'd done to them.

But I couldn't imagine how they could ever look at me with love and respect ever again, and I feared when Chase opened his eyes all I would see would be resentment and anger.

Danny finally came into the room and looked alarmed at my tear-stained face. I had been terrified to move, and I could feel the snot and tears drying and crusting my skin as I sat as still as a statue.

He gathered me into his arms, wiping my face with his sleeve. "The kids will both be here tomorrow morning, Livvie. Don't cry. This is a happy time, Lu. We finally have our boy back, and we're never going to let him go ever again. I promise."

I nodded, burying my face in the warmth of his chest as I allowed the strength of his arms to protect me. I pushed down the fear that once Chase woke up, he would reject me. I wanted to have hope.

I wanted to believe that he might be able to forgive me for everything I had done to him.

Even if it was just for a moment.

CHAPTER FOURTEEN

Olivia, Age Seven
Molly, Age Fourteen

OLIVIA STOOD FROZEN.

She had desperately been trying to stay away from Roger, but when she got home from school, Molly wasn't waiting for her like she usually was. Roger sat in the worn out armchair that reminded her faintly of the father she carefully remembered.

"Hi there, Princess," Roger greeted her as she walked in the door.

She thought about turning around and running back out, but her body refused to move. The way he was smiling at her made her skin crawl.

"W-W-Where is M-M-Mommy?" she asked, her voice barely audible.

"She's with Molly. Your stupid sister got in trouble at school because she got into another fight. She may be expelled for good this time."

"Molly isn't here either?" Olivia asked, alarms going off in her head.

"No, Princess. It looks like it's finally just you and me." Roger patted his knee. "Why don't you come and sit on my lap and tell me about what happened at school."

Olivia's feet felt cemented to the floor.

"I have homework," she muttered.

"Come on, it can't hurt to come and talk to me for a few minutes." Roger's voice was nicer than she'd ever heard it. Too nice, and it made Olivia feel nauseous.

"I have homework," she repeated.

"I said come and tell me about school. Now!" Olivia jumped as he yelled.

She walked slowly to where he sat, looking back at the door and wishing desperately that Molly would come through it at any time. Molly had promised to protect her, and right now she felt she might need some protection.

"Hurry it up, Princess. We don't have all day," Roger said, harshly.

As she approached him, he reached over and grabbed her around the waist, pulling her up on his lap in one rough motion.

"There. That's not so bad, is it?" Roger asked, his breath hot on her cheek as he pulled her closer to him.

Olivia winced as the smell of stale beer and cigarettes mingled with his body odor. She tried not to gag, afraid to make him angry with her.

She shook her head, careful not to make eye contact.

"Good. Now lean back against your Uncle Roger, and tell me about your day. We never get a chance to talk because of those other women that are always hovering around. I've been wanting to get to know you for a long time." Olivia felt him pull her closer against him, his arm strong against her waist. She felt trapped and tried not to panic.

"It was fine. Good," she said, her voice barely above a whisper.

"Come now, there has to be more to tell." He reached up and stroked her hair with fat, dirty fingers. "Don't you have more to tell Uncle Roger?"

Olivia squirmed and realized she couldn't move, her body pinned against his. His breathing was becoming faster as he began to stroke her hair harder.

"Please... let me go," Olivia whimpered.

"Where do you want to go?" Roger asked, his face close against hers. She could almost see the mist coming from his mouth, his lips wet and disgusting. "I think you're fine, right here."

His fat fingers moved to her cheek as he ran his finger down the side of her cheek and down her neck to the collar of her shirt.

"Please..." Olivia cried out.

The door to the trailer suddenly flew open and Molly ran in, rage in her eyes.

"Let her go right now, you disgusting pervert!" she screamed.

Roger froze, but instead of letting her go, squeezed Olivia harder.

"I'm not doing anything wrong, Psycho. Olivia and I are just getting to know one another a little better." Roger grinned.

"I said, let her go. Right now." Molly stepped toward the chair, unafraid.

They stared at one another until Olivia felt Roger release her slowly.

"Are you okay, Livvie?" Molly said, looking down at her for a moment.

"Yes, I-I-I" Olivia suddenly felt herself fly across the room as Roger charged Molly, knocking her flat on her back.

Olivia lay on the ground, unable to move as she heard Roger swearing. She could hear Molly crying out. She heard glass breaking and wood splintering as she struggled to stand, blood running down the side of her face. She heard the familiar sound of slapping and kicking until finally she heard nothing but the sound of heavy breathing.

"Get up, Molly. Quit pretending like you're hurt. Get up right now before your momma gets home." Roger panted.

Olivia strained to hear movement, but there was nothing but silence.

"I said, 'get up'!" Roger's voice was strained. "Oh sweet Jesus. What have I done?"

Olivia's heart began to beat hard in her chest as she waited for the sound of Molly's voice, but she heard nothing. She tried to wipe the blood away from the side of her face, but it kept flowing. She was terrified to move or even breathe as she prayed to hear the sound of Molly's voice, but the only sound she heard was Rogers cries.

"What have I done? Oh God, what have I done?"

CHAPTER FIFTEEN

Olivia, Age Forty-Six

THE LEAVES WERE NEARLY GONE from the trees, and the wind was turning colder the day that Danny moved back home. It was the same type of day when Danny moved out three years earlier. Only this day was filled with excitement and happiness, not grief and loss like it had been when he left.

Life had come full circle, and for the first time, hope was growing within me slowly and cautiously. But I could feel it spreading inside of me, against my will.

Jill and Chase came home for Thanksgiving break, and both instantly knew the moment they walked into the house that something was different. We had decided to surprise them when they came home, knowing how much they both loved surprises.

Jill had gotten home a day earlier than she planned, her little blue Focus full of dirty laundry and books haphazardly scattered throughout the back seat. I could hear her voice calling my name before the car even came to a stop. I had been on the porch smoking, even though I had promised myself that I would stop. As she got out, her eyes rested on Danny's truck that was parked in the drive in its old spot instead of on the street where he had been parking for the past few years.

"Mom," Jill's voice was filled with subtle hope and confusion. "Why... is Dad's car in the driveway? What's it..."

Danny stepped out onto the porch, put his arm around my waist and gave Jill a meaningful grin.

"Wait... what?" Jill dropped her purse and ran to us, practically jumping into our arms. "Are you... is this... are you?"

"Come and sit," Danny said, pulling her into the house while I stubbed out the last of my cigarette.

We sat together in front of the fire and explained the events of the last month, Jill's beautiful blue eyes growing larger as we spoke, both of us taking turns talking. The sparkle in her eyes grew in the firelight, and I hoped she would never lose that as she became the woman she was growing into.

"You two are shitting me!" Jill said finally as she flopped back against the deep chair she had been sitting in, a frown spreading across her face. "I can't believe that with everything we've been through you've ended up back together! Who does that?"

"Are you happy?" Danny asked, both of us confused by the sudden change in her expression.

"Of course, I'm happy! But what happens when the next bad thing happens? Will you two split up again?" Jill asked, her tone turning to a far-too familiar one; one that I had used with her many times before.

"Jilly, its more complicated than that. We didn't just split up. There was more to it." I said, trying not to sound defensive.

"I know, Mom, but I'm just trying to be real about this. I don't want to get excited about it only to watch you break up again. You have to understand what I'm saying," She seemed as though she was the adult and I was the child, and I wondered if she might be right.

"Listen, Jilly," Danny said, stepping in to save me. "There aren't always guarantees, but one thing that had never changed is that I love your mom and she loves me. You've made some valid points, but sometimes there just aren't answers, and you just have to work through it, take the chance and try anyway."

Jill sat silently, and I understood that she had been hurt, too. When Danny moved out, it devastated her like everyone else, and she had borne the brunt of it, often sleeping in my bed, both of us crying ourselves to sleep. She missed him the most, and the pain in my heart reminded me that we had hurt her, too.

"I'm sorry, Jilly. We didn't mean to hurt you with our problems. It's just..."

"It's just that you two are just as messed up as everyone else in this effed up world," Ben's voice made everyone startle as we realized that he had suddenly materialized in the room.

"Benji!" Jill jumped up and ran to her older brother, grabbing him in a huge bear hug. It had been months since they'd seen each other last.

"Hi, sweetie," I said, so happy to see him.

"Hi, Mom," Ben said, walking over and enveloping me in a tight squeeze. He towered over me, long and lean like Danny. I could smell his cologne and I was reminded that he was a man now and not the little boy I had adored so much. I held him for a long time, unable to let go.

I finally released him and tried to wipe the tears that fell down my cheeks without anyone seeing until I realized that his were wet as well.

"I've missed you," Ben said, smiling, his dark brown eyes warm and soft.

"I've missed you too, buddy," I said hugging him and Jill, happy that we were almost all together. But no matter how close I held them, I couldn't bring them close enough to make me forget that about how much I had hurt them.

Danny stepped in, waiting patiently as he usually did.

"Do you have a hug for your old dad?" he asked, grabbing Ben and pulling him in for a strong hug.

Ben, the oldest child, the first son and the athlete. He and Danny had always been close since the first day of tee-ball and their connection was strong and evident

Jill had belonged to all of us but Chase had always been my baby, at least until I had nearly destroyed him. Even after that, he still clung to me for reasons I wasn't sure of. I never knew if it was out of love, or fear of me dying, but I always liked to believe it was love.

Chase stood in the hallway silently waiting for his brother and sister to notice him. Jill turned his direction and suddenly screamed.

"Oh my God, you're home!" she ran to him as hard as she could and body-tackled him, knocking him to the ground.

It was a far different greeting than when they had been reunited in the hospital over a month before. Both Jill and Ben had raced from school to the hospital to see him, but he had been lethargic and uninterested.

"Mom, what is wrong with him?" Jill had tears in her eyes, her disappointment breaking my heart.

"He's just... been through a lot, Jill. It's going to take him time to heal... and recover. It's going to take us all some time."

Ben's reaction hadn't been any better, both of them driving hours to be met with their brother's indifference.

They had both gone back to school a couple of days later trying to swallow the bitterness and disappointment. In spite of it all, they remained his biggest cheerleaders, even coming home for some of the family sessions at the facility.

"Yes! I'm home, for good," Chase said, laughing.

Ben reached over and helped him up, pulling him into a bear hug. "You look good, bro."

Chase smiled self-consciously.

He did look good. He'd put on a bit of weight and his skin had returned to a healthier shade. His smile had even returned, and in spite of everything he had been through, I could still see my beautiful little boy in his eyes.

We spent the evening catching up, talking late into the night. It was the first time we had been together in so long, but it was as though not a moment had ever passed. Jill caught us up on the adventures of freshman life, and Ben dazzled us with his maturity and newfound views on life that came only from being away from home.

"I'm so tired," I said finally, unable to keep my eyes open. "I must lie down."

"I'll go with you," Danny said, kissing me on the cheek. I leaned my head against him and sighed. For the first time that I could remember, I was happy.

Truly happy.

I took Danny's advice and instead of fighting against it, I embraced it, finally feeling at peace.

I kissed each of my children on the top of their heads, and whispered "I love you," into their ears. Then I promised myself that I would always do everything in my power to be good to them and to fight to be the mother and wife who was deserving of every wonderful thing that there was in my life.

Danny and I walked hand in hand to our bedroom, and I promised myself that I would finally be good to myself, too.

CHAPTER SIXTEEN

Olivia, Age Forty-Seven

MOLLY!

I could see, and I wondered if I was awake or in a dream, but I could see her as clearly as the hand in front of my face.

Impossible!

I watched as the fat man threw her across the room.

I couldn't believe that I had forgotten all about him. He had been the one Mommy had let move in with us for a short time. As I looked at him now, I felt sick to my stomach as I remembered how he used to look at me, making me feel completely bare. His greasy face made me feel nauseous, and suddenly the memory of his fat fingers on my face overwhelmed me.

I could feel his hot breath on my cheek and smell his breath, instantly making me want to vomit.

I watched in horror as he threw Molly across the room

in slow motion. Fear overcame me as she hit her head on the side of the end table, the blood flowing immediately.

I suddenly understood that she had been protecting me. From him.

I watched as she lay motionless. I felt as though I was floating as I watched a much younger version of me run to her and begin shaking her.

"Molly, no!!! Wake up, Molly. Wake up!" I cried. I could feel the tears running down my face, my heart breaking into a thousand pieces as helplessness began to crush me.

Blood flowed from her head, her face turning white.

I watched as Mommy suddenly appeared and picked up a heavy ashtray. She hit Roger over the head, knocking him over as sirens began to sound in the background, getting louder with each passing moment.

I leaned over Molly, my hands on her face.

"Wake up, Molly, please. Wake up."

Molly's head moved slightly, her eyes closed. As I watched her lips start to move, I leaned in closer to hear her.

"I love you... I'm sorry."

"No, please. I need you," I cried, everything in me wanting for her to open her eyes. "You can't leave me. I can't live without you."

"I'm sorry." Molly's voice was faint, and I put my cheek against hers, feeling the coolness of it on mine.

I could feel someone grabbing my arm, but I refused to let go of her.

"We need to go, Olivia!" Mommy's voice was panicked, the sirens on top of us. "We need to go now!"

The door to the trailer slammed open and footsteps echoed throughout the tiny space.

"Don't move!"

Mommy's hands flew up in the air as she dropped to the ground.

"What happened?" A police officer looked around the room at the blood and the two bodies on the floor.

"They did it," I heard myself cry, lifting my head for a moment to stare at Mommy. "My Mommy and Roger did this to her."

"Get the kid," I heard someone yell. I laid my head down and held tight to Molly.

"Leave me alone!" I cried.

"Please come with us, kid."

"No! I'm not leaving my sister! Leave me alone!" I screamed as gentle hands tried to pry me away from Molly's lifeless body. I buried my head in her chest convinced that I would never open my eyes again.

"Please, let go. She's gone. It's okay. Let her go," the voice was familiar but I couldn't bring myself to loosen my hold.

"I can't let her go! She's everything to me. I can't," I cried.

"She would want you to let her go, Livvie. She would want you to live your life. She did everything she could to protect you because she loved you more than anything in the world. You know this now. Let her go."

"If I let her go then she'll disappear forever, and I can't lose her," I lifted my head as I looked for the voice, tears flowing non-stop down my face.

I was stunned to see Danny and Dr. Sullivan in front of me, and as I looked down to touch Molly, she disappeared before my eyes.

"Oh my God, where is she?" I cried, my chest heaving as I looked frantically around the room.

"It's okay, Lu... it's okay," Danny tried to hide the guilt

in his eyes before he pulled me tight against his chest. "It's okay. She's been gone for a long time."

"I know," I cried, pushing him away. I didn't want to be close to him. Just as we were getting even closer, I couldn't understand why he'd do this to me. I was crushed as I felt her loss all over again. "Why? What did you do to me?"

I began sobbing, unable to catch my breath, the depths of my sorrow unimaginable.

"She died... protecting me. She died because she loved me." The words barely came out as I sank to the floor. "If it wasn't for me, she would still be alive. My mother let him kill Molly. I could finally see it."

Danny slowly crept toward me, his arms open but I refused to give in.

"Why would you let me see her again only to take her from me? Didn't you know that it would destroy me? How could you not know? I hugged myself tight trying desperately to forget the pain.

"I'm sorry, Lu... I thought you... I wanted you... "

"You wanted to see... you needed to see what happened. How it all happened," Dr. Sullivan's voice was crisp and business-like. "You asked for this, Olivia."

It was the first time she'd said a word, and my tears stopped almost instantly.

"This was me? I wanted this?" I knew she was telling the truth. I'd been searching for this my entire life and never believed that I could ever know. But now that I did... I realized that some of the biggest parts of my life had been a lie.

Cynthia and Lou had both lied to me. I knew that I should've known, but I'd had one last hope that I could believe one thing they'd said to me.

Every truth in my life had been based on the fact that the one person I'd loved the most had tried to hurt me, and knowing that she'd given her life for me changed everything for reasons I couldn't explain.

"Things can be different now," I said to Danny, holding him close. "I can't explain it to you but I know it. Knowing that she loved me... gave her life for me, gives me everything in life that I need."

Danny kissed the top of my head and pulled me in for tight hug.

"I'm so glad, Olivia. I so happy that you can finally see it for yourself."

"See what?" I said, kissing him on the cheek.

"That you've always been worthy... you've always been amazing and beautiful and strong enough." He kissed me softly on the lips. "Molly loved you for the same reasons the rest of us love you. Because Livvie-Lu... you're the good one."

The End

AFTERWORD

Thank you so much for reading The Good One, Part Two!

Please help others to find my book by leaving an honest review on Goodreads or on your favorite book-buying platform.

Reviews don't have to be long or detailed. They can be one or two lines that simply state how you felt about the book! It helps readers want to take a chance on a new-to-them author and we appreciate it so very much!

If you'd like to keep up with me, please join my email list and you'll receive a free eCopy of Leaving Eva, the first book in the Eva Series, as well as updates and news about my author journey.

Thank you so much for reading!

X,

Jennifer

ACKNOWLEDGMENTS

A book is never written by one single person.

The words on the page are mine, but the motivation, the cover, the polish, and the story development are a result of my beautiful Tribe.

I am so thankful for my mom who reads every word that I write and encourages me to continue. I realize how lucky I am to have family who supports me so much.

I am so fortunate to have such incredible readers who have become friends, and then become integral to the publishing process like Karen Hoy. She encourages, motivates, and gives me feedback on every story that I write. I am so incredibly thankful for that I met her in Toledo and that she took a chance on this author she had never heard of before.

JC Wing, my wonderful editor gives me such happiness and joy and having her in my life is truly a blessing.

Lastly but never least, none of this would mean anything without my incredible family who gives me the space and time to create and publish these stories that live inside my head and heart. They are only possible because you allow them to be.

ALSO BY JENNIFER SIVEC

Leaving Eva

Losing Eva

Saving Eva

The Eva Series; the Complete Collection

I Run to You

The Forgotten

The Other Half of Me

The Good One, Part One

The Good One, Part Two

Grey's Harbor Series:

Grey's Landing (Book One)-Lark Griffing

The Grey's Harbor Anthology (Book Two)-JC Wing, Piper Malone, Carol Cassada, Lark Griffing, Jennifer Sivec

Hope Adrift (Book Three)-Lark Griffing

Harbor Tides (Book Four)-Lark Griffing

Perfect Seas (Book Five)-Jennifer Sivec

(Harbor Song (Book Six)-JC Wing)

A Grey's Harbor Christmas Anthology (Book Seven)-JC Wing, Lark Griffing, Piper Malone, Jennifer Sivec

ABOUT THE AUTHOR

Jennifer Sivec writes beautifully broken stories with heart.

She is attracted to and writes stories with characters that are complicated, flawed and completely imperfect. Her books are often a reflection of life, encompassing difficult subjects such as cancer, addiction, abandonment, and abuse. She writes with a raw, complex, yet hopeful approach often weaving tragic stories with honesty and

grace, creating unforgettable characters.

Jennifer's passion for reading and sharing stories gives her perspective and peace of mind.

She lives in Ohio with her husband, two boys, herd of dogs who create balance and levity for her. She loves her crazy life and wonderful readers, and is grateful for all of it, every day.